LET SLEEPING DOGS LIE

CYNTHIA TERELST

ISBN: 978-0-6487294-1-9

 Created with Vellum

Thank you to everyone who has supported me and my love of writing. For those who read early drafts and helped me bring another novel to fruition, I could not do this without you, you are all invaluable to me.

PROLOGUE

THE CHRISTMAS I WAS SEVEN, Zac sent me on a wild scavenger hunt up and down our street, leaving clue after clue for me. It led me straight back to my bedroom, where a large box sat in the middle of the floor.

I stood there staring at it, wondering what my next clue would be. If I'd completed the hunt, Zac would have been there to congratulate me. That was our custom. Peeking over my shoulder, I searched the hallway for him. Nothing. Satisfied that my next clue awaited me in the box, I strode over to it and flipped the lid open.

Quick as a flash, something brown rushed at my face. Stumbling back, I let out a cry. My parents appeared behind me, their voices filled with joy. I didn't hear what they were saying. I couldn't comprehend a word. All I could do was stare at the bundle of fur Zac was holding, looking straight back at me. A bundle of fur in the form of a puppy.

Zac was grinning from ear to ear, his blond hair ruffled, his face covered in a sheen of sweat from being in the box.

"Merry Christmas, Tara," he said, his voice high in excitement. I took the puppy in my arms. To this day, Benny was the most amazing gift I'd ever received.

That was the last Christmas with our parents.

TWENTY DAYS

Tara

DEAR TARA,

Congratulations! Your application for the inaugural Millionaire Scavenger Hunt has been accepted. The winning team will be awarded $6 million.

To accept your position, please forward your $200,000 entry fee within 72 hours of receiving this email.

The hunt will take place in a secret location. Please arrive at Tullamarine Airport at 9am on 6 April, at which time we will text you further instructions.

Thank you for your interest and good luck.

I STOOD in the airport terminal reading the email for the hundredth time. When I'd received the invitation a month ago, I thoroughly investigated the details. $200,000 was a lot to invest in something that could be a lie. The money for our entry fees was held in a trust fund, and a prominent law firm held the deed for that fund. The organisation running the hunt was legitimate. Once I knew everything was above board, I had no hesitation in entering.

I had no idea where I was going or how long my flight would be, so I wore comfy tracky dacks and a loose t-shirt. It wasn't 9am yet. There were still two long minutes before the text would arrive. I folded the printed email and put it in my backpack. Excitement rushed through me like it had when I'd received the acceptance letter. Two hundred thousand dollars was a big risk and the thought I might lose all that money gave me a headache if I thought about it for too long. But the invitation said I could win a minimum of one million dollars. What I could do with that money outweighed the risk for me. I could run my foundation for at least five years.

But it wasn't just the money. I felt called to join the hunt. It was everything a scavenger hunt meant to me.

For the past few years, life had been flat. Losing Zac changed everything. My ability to trust in life and love diminished. After Zac died, I had gotten close to someone, once. Only once. I learnt my lesson about what fate thought about life and love.

As I went through the motions of the life I'd made for myself, every day was just like every other day. I needed to feel something, anything. The thrill of the hunt could fill that empty space. It could make me live in the moment.

The crowd bustled around me. Any of these people could be one of my partners. The middle-aged Asian man speaking Mandarin, the most widely spoken language on the planet, would be a bonus. The old grey-haired man, getting help with his computerised check-in, could bring years of knowledge. Excited chatting beside me drew my attention to a girl in her late teens. She was animated in both voice and body language. Her enthusiasm could help drive a team. Everyone here could be of benefit and offer strength and talent. But none more than my brother Zac would have.

A scavenger hunt would have excited Zac, more than anything.

Memories were precious, but I needed to concentrate on the game at hand. I looked back around at the crowd. Back at the people I'd noticed earlier. What could their weaknesses be? The point of looking at weaknesses was not to be negative, but to see how others could prop them up. The man who spoke fluent Mandarin was dressed in an impeccable suit. Perhaps he was not accustomed to working outside the office environment. The old man though, his hands looked like they had seen many a day of hard work. He could help the other man adjust. That same old man who has trouble with technology could learn from the teen. And in turn, they could both settle her flightiness. Winning was about teamwork.

I scanned the crowd further. There was a group of guys standing together laughing, joking around. If it wasn't the first half of the year, I'd think they were from a football club and heading off for Mad Monday. Their distraction, their complete and utter manliness, would not make them good team members. It would be hard work keeping even one of them in line.

My phone beeped, bringing me out of my reverie.

Welcome to the game, Tara. Your ticket is attached. Please board flight 3692 to Sydney. When you arrive, a driver will take you to Hotel Cosmos to meet your partner.

Partner. Not *partners*. That meant the prize would be split between two of us. I thought about what three million dollars would mean. I would use it to help vulnerable young Australians avoid Zac's fate. It would allow me to honour the memory of the brother I loved dearly and lost too soon.

Shepherd

I SAT IN THE APARTMENT, waiting. Sitting would be an exaggeration, seeing that every two minutes, I wrestled the stillness and got up to pace. The grey carpet beneath my feet was sensible apartment carpet, designed for high traffic areas. The blue plush rug under the coffee table gave it some softness. The navy couches were surprisingly soft even though they weren't lavish leather.

I chose Hotel Cosmos because it was split into hotel rooms on the lower floors and apartments on the higher levels. Tara would be more comfortable having a bedroom to herself. It was important that she felt comfortable if this was going to work. Otherwise this whole thing would be like pushing shit uphill...with open fingers.

I flicked through the Sydney visitor guide on the table, not taking in any of the pictures or words.

Tara landed forty minutes ago, her arrival at the hotel was imminent. How would I feel seeing her again after five years? More to the point, how would *she* feel?

One day she was there, ready to take on life with me, celebrating our completion of grad school. The next, she was gone. No explanation. No note. Nothing.

I brushed it off. Pretended it didn't matter. I partied and drowned my sorrows in more ways than one. But it didn't make a difference. I could try to deny it. Reality always came back to me. Sometimes it niggled at me. Sometimes it smashed me in the face like a freight train hurtling at a hundred miles an hour. She was gone and no matter how many years passed I still missed her.

The twelve months I'd spent with her at grad school, I had grown to love her in so many ways. It wasn't just the way she believed in me and helped me grow. I shared things with her I'd never shared with anyone – my dreams and plans. I didn't have to hide who I was when I was with her. She told me how happy I made her, how I made her feel special and loved. I never understood why she left me.

Life without her was hollow. I didn't want to live like that anymore.

So, I concocted this game, this million-dollar scavenger hunt. I hoped she wouldn't be able to resist. Scavenger hunts, mazes, puzzles, were her thing. I'd worded the invitation in a way I knew would appeal to her. It was exactly the way she described scavenger hunts to me. I used the words she did – challenge, turning on cognitive thought processes, the thrill of solving the puzzle, learning about strengths and weaknesses. And to top it off, there was a tempting prize.

Sammy, my best friend since we were in diapers, said it was a bad idea. I can still remember the conversation.

"SHEPHERD, IT'S BEEN FIVE YEARS."

Did he think I was stupid? I knew exactly how long it had been.

Sammy didn't wait for a reply. "Can't you just speak to her like a normal person?"

"I don't think that will work."

He let out an exasperated breath and raised his eyes skyward, maybe asking for divine intervention. "Why, because you're not normal?"

"She's not exactly here to talk to, is she?"

"There's a thing called a phone." Sammy was good at this sarcastic shit.

"And when she hangs up on me, then what? This is better. She will apply for the hunt; I'm sure she will."

"And then what? She'll magically fall in love with you again?"

It sounded stupid when he said it.

"Maybe."

"You don't think she's going to be pissed when she finds out it's all a ruse?"

"No. Why would she?"

I swear if he were closer to me, he would have slapped me upside of the head. "You're delusional."

"So, you'll help me then?"

"Yes, I'll help you." He sighed like a teenager being asked to take out the trash.

NOW, as I sat in the apartment waiting for Tara, I heard the lock click. I sat still, clenching my hands. Only my eyes moved as she walked into the room. They devoured every inch of her. She was as beautiful as the last time I saw her, even in sweatpants and a t-shirt. My stomach knotted. She stirred things inside me like no one else ever could.

Tara's green eyes opened wide, and she stopped dead in

her tracks the moment she laid eyes on me. Her face hardened.

"You've got to be fucking kidding me."

She looked like she had just been kicked.

Maybe I should have tried to speak to her...like a normal person, on the phone.

<hr>

Tara

I STOOD THERE, inside the entry, as the door closed behind me. My stomach dropped. I had not seen Shepherd Bell III in five years. Not since graduation day when I turned up to his share house.

I was expecting a party, yes. But what I found went far beyond that. And there was Shepherd in the middle of it all, chugging beers, as high as a kite. I don't know how long I stood in the hallway, watching him. My body was frozen, except for the shaking and the bile rising in my throat. I couldn't reconcile what I was seeing with the Shepherd I knew, the Shepherd I loved. I didn't want to believe it, but he was right there in front of my eyes.

Shepherd's face was replaced with Zac's. This was exactly how it started with Zac, my normally reserved brother standing on stage, the centre of attention, flaunting himself. I took hold of the door jamb. The rigidness of the wood under my palm steadied my turmoil. I pushed off it, turned around and never looked back. It was not something I needed to live through. Again.

Should I have explained myself? Maybe. Should I have

given him a chance? Maybe. It was something I'd thought about over the last five years. But I'd learnt to live with my decision. I preferred to think his actions had made the decision for me.

I needed to look for signs now. I could not be around him if he was doing drugs.

Shepherd rose and made his way towards me, while I stood with my back against the door. He wiped his palms down the front of his jeans. I knew that action. Nerves made his hands sweaty.

My traitorous heart beat faster at his approach. I tried not to notice how his t-shirt fit against his wide chest and shoulders or how his jeans hugged his legs. His build may have filled out, but apart from that he looked the same as I remembered him. Tall, with brown tousled hair, warm brown eyes, and tanned skin. I'm sure the killer-smile would have been the same too, although right then his smile was tentative.

"Hi, Tara." His tone was low, apprehensive. He stopped two metres away from me. It was a deliberate move; a tactic we learnt in dispute resolution at graduate school. Don't crowd the opposition.

"Shepherd."

His smile widened. My stomach tightened. I couldn't believe he still had such an effect on me after all these years apart.

"You look great," he said.

"Thanks." What else was I going to say? 'You look great too?' He did, but I wasn't about to tell him that.

Out of all the people on this scavenger hunt, how did I get paired with Shepherd? What were the chances? If this was fate playing games with me, then fate sucked.

Coming closer, he handed me an envelope, his hand steady. "The rules."

"Have you read them?" I said, grasping the envelope by the corner.

He nodded, giving me a half smile. That half smile made me nervous. There must have been something in the rules I wouldn't like. I took the envelope from him and sat on the blue two-seater lounge. He sat on the arm of the other lounge, watching me. I tried to keep my face placid, but as I read the first rule, my teeth clenched.

You must stay together at all times.

Great. I had successfully stayed away from Shepherd for five years, to save myself from a fate worse than death. And now I needed to spend every moment with him? I shook my head. I didn't look up at Shepherd. I didn't want to see his reaction.

This was going to be hard. Mentally, physically, and emotionally.

There are five hunts you need to complete within twenty days. The first team to finish wins. If you finish the hunt early, you need to stay together for the allotted time period to give other teams a chance to complete it without interference.

"Do you think it's weird that we have to stay together for twenty days, even if we finish early?" I asked Shepherd, raising my eyes to him.

"Maybe."

I screwed my face up at his non-commitment.

Twenty days. I knew that, of course. It had been in the initial invite. But it took on a whole new dimension when I knew I had to spend every moment with Shepherd for twenty days. Once, it would have been a dream come true.

Now? Not so much.

I was happy with my life. It was fulfilling. I helped people. I didn't need to be distracted from my goal. And Shepherd would be a distraction.

Were the other teams completing the same hunts as us? How many other teams were there? Not knowing the opposition was a distinct disadvantage. We didn't know their strengths and weaknesses. We were completely blind. But in another way, it was an advantage because we would concentrate on our own game.

You can search online, but you cannot directly ask for outside help, except when you reach your destination. You will download an app to your electronic devices to monitor use. Points will be deducted for each offence.

That would be easy enough. Shepherd and I were both smart. I was sure we could figure out the clues together. We'd studied together night after night, researching case law for our assignments, drilling down and investigating clause after clause, verdict after verdict, argument after argument.

I knew Shepherd was studying me closely. My skin tingled, as it always had, when he watched me. Unsettling butterflies fluttered around my insides. Why did he have to look at me like that? Why did he have to look at me at all? I glanced up at him, my lips pursed, before turning my eyes back to the page.

Your spending limit is five thousand dollars. All expenses must be paid from this. The credit card is in the envelope.

"What's so funny?" Shepherd asked.

Oh crap, I must have actually laughed out loud.

"Nothing." I squirmed in my seat.

How was Shepherd going to cope? The man was born with a silver spoon in his mouth. Shepherd lived in a mansion, drove a BMW, and received a trust fund payment every year.

But that was not being fair. He may have been born into money but he never acted like an entitled rich kid. He didn't waste money like it grew on trees. Wait, why was I defending him? I needed to think of Shepherd as my team mate. Nothing more, nothing less. He was the person who would help me win three million for my foundation. For Zac.

You will be disqualified if you break the law.

That would be an easy rule for me to follow. I was pretty sure it wouldn't be hard for Shepherd, either. After all, we were both lawyers and that should mean we were averse to breaking the law. The only time I'd known him to break the law was when he took illicit drugs. Hopefully, he'd grown out of that. Although, some of those from old money never grew out of it.

I knew money could ruin a person. It could go to their head and I was determined that would never happen to me. Despite being a millionaire, I tried not to immerse myself in the millionaire lifestyle. I didn't dress in designer clothes and eat at fancy restaurants where three scallops on a plate cost fifty dollars.

My money was not old money. It came from Zac, from his intuitiveness. I used it in memory of him. All of my work was pro bono. I didn't make millions every year and I didn't have rich clients I could ask for donations. That's why I needed to win this hunt. My money would last a lifetime because I was conservative with it, but I couldn't afford to keep a foundation running off it. I couldn't afford to lose two hundred thousand either, but now was not the time to think about that.

You must remain polite and courteous to strangers and team members at all times. If you are found to be harassing or abusive, you will be disqualified.

I could do that. How hard could it be? Shepherd and I didn't end on bad terms. We just ended. Abruptly. Forever. Because of his reckless behaviour.

Photographs or videos must be taken to verify your finds.

Easy. I couldn't see a problem with that.

The judge's decision will be final.

Final. I broke out into a sweat. I don't know why it had taken until now for the full realisation of the risk I was taking to hit me. I could lose two hundred thousand dollars, because, for some strange reason, I felt compelled to join a scavenger hunt.

I looked up at Shepherd. I needed him to know this wasn't just a game to me. Winning could change the lives of many people. It could *save* the lives of many people. Shepherd looked back at me. His face neutral as his eyes searched mine. The bloody butterflies wouldn't settle.

Shepherd

TARA'S FACE WAS STERN. The furrow between her eyes was the one that always appeared when she was deep in thought and consideration. But she hadn't smiled once since she entered the room. That was unlike the Tara I knew.

"I hope you're going to take this seriously. This is not just a game for me."

What did she mean? My goal, the way I'd planned it out in my head, is that we'd have fun. We'd get close again. She would fall in love with me again and would no longer be the one who got away, because I would have her back. When I didn't reply, she continued. "I need this money, Shepherd. It will be the start-up money for my foundation."

Fuck. What? There wasn't a prize of six million dollars.

We were the only two people in the game. There was her two hundred thousand, which I was going to give back. But she was relying on three million. Where the hell was I going to get three million dollars?

"What foundation?" I managed to ask.

"The Zachariah Hill Foundation. It's in memory of my brother."

Her brother? I knew she had a brother. She often spoke about their childhood and the scavenger hunts they'd done. They even did them at university in Australia, before she came to the States for grad school. They set up a club and had regular hunts with other students. When did he die? I had read nothing about it in the five years since she left me.

"What will the foundation do?" It would be good work, important work. Everything Tara did was good and important.

"It will help vulnerable young adults—the LGBTQ, indigenous, mentally ill, foster care children, or anyone who needs help to stay away from drugs."

I knew it. "How will it help them?"

"Through an outreach van. If we win this money, I can have a van for the inner city and three more vans to cover the north, east and western suburbs, meaning we can help more people. I was only going to be able to afford one van until this competition came along. Imagine what a difference the foundation could make with three million dollars."

This was not good. I couldn't let her down. I needed to find the money somehow.

I had watched her over the years from half a world away, and I knew she helped many underprivileged clients. This foundation would just add to the list. She had done work overseas, helping those in society who had no way of helping themselves; they couldn't take on corporations or their oppressors. They were uneducated, scared, and helpless. And there she was, trying to make the world a better place for them.

I tried to be more like her: selfless, strong, determined. It was the person I'd always wanted to be deep down and she had believed in me enough that I believed I could do it. I had convinced my father to allow me to take on some cases that wouldn't bring in money, but would help people regain their lives. Now would be my chance to prove I could be as selfless as her. I would raise that $3 million, for her and her foundation. No ties attached.

"If we are going to get this money, let's download these apps and get our first clue," I said, taking my phone out of my pocket. I deliberately avoided the word *win*. I may have made up this game, but I didn't want to add straight out lying to the mix.

Tara

"I'M GOING to need a few minutes to settle in. Which way is my room?"

Shepherd pointed to the left and I started to pull my suitcase after me. Shit, it was heavy. I had packed for every possible climate. If only I had known Sydney was the destination, I would have packed lighter. Who am I kidding? I would have just packed for more scenarios instead: dancing, hiking, swimming. Who knows what the organisers had in store for us?

"Do you want some help with that?" Shepherd asked.

Yes. "No, I'll be fine, thanks."

The room was pleasant enough – the grey carpet from the living area flowed through. The walls were light grey and a huge black and white photo of a border collie hung above the queen size bed. The furniture was simple but elegant in beech. The only real colour came from the red throw and the red cushions on the bed. I sank down onto the bed and stared at the wall.

What was Shepherd doing here? Since when did he like scavenger hunts? I didn't want to be paired with him. It would bring back too many memories. Was there any way I could get out of this? All of the teams would have already been allocated and asking for a swap was likely impossible. Withdrawing was not an option because I'd lose my $200,000.

How bad could it really be? I didn't *hate* Shepherd. He wasn't a bad person.

I walked into the bathroom and splashed water on my face. I could do this. We could win six million dollars. I could start the foundation and keep it running for years. I stared myself down in the mirror. Solved. I nodded to myself and headed back out to the living area. My new mantra was going to be 'don't get too close, and make sure he's not taking drugs.'

Shepherd looked up at me expectantly. I gave him a half-hearted smile. "OK. Let's get this show on the road. What's the app I need to download?"

"The Scavenger Monitoring App."

As soon as it was downloaded, the first clues came in. I joined Shepherd at the dining room table and read them out.

<u>**Hunt 1**</u>
Nobody knows how many people
died here.
It was the last place many people
saw after arriving in Australia.
The grave diggers did not keep
detailed records, and some
bodies were buried in unmarked
graves on a hillside, at the
bottom of which was the water
supply.
Visit the home of the gravediggers to
find your first item. The only way
to find it is in the dark.

"Have you got any ideas what the clues are directing us to?" Shepherd asked.

"Not the slightest. Being from Melbourne, I don't know a lot about Sydney. I know the major landmarks like the Bridge, Opera House and Bondi Beach. It would be like asking someone from LA if they knew much about Chicago."

"No benefit for us then that you're Australian."

"Except I know the language and how things work."

"We both speak English." His resigned smile showed me he knew what I meant. He laughed. "Yeah. OK. I don't speak Australian."

"Exactly. If I said to you, 'Hey cobber, chuck a u-ey up there so we can go to the servo,' would you know what I meant?"

Shepherd's eyebrows drew together. "Nope."

"It means 'Make a U-turn at the next intersection so we can go to the gas station.'"

"Of course it does, because why would you want to go to the effort of saying U-turn?"

He had no idea.

"Or maybe we could go to Maccas in the arvo for a cuppa."

"We're going to McDonalds for what?" Shepherd shook his head.

"We could have a bickie too."

He took a long, drawn breath in.

"C'mon, you're in Straya now."

I laughed as Shepherd shook his head, rolling his eyes. Clear eyes, not glassy, not bloodshot. Of course, he wouldn't know what a *cuppa* is, neither of us were coffee or tea drinkers so I'd never used the term with him before. But he did remember what *Maccas* meant. I bit my lip to withhold my smile.

"I said, 'Maybe we could go to McDonald's in the afternoon for a cup of tea and a biscuit, too.'"

"You did not say that."

"We Australians don't like to use more syllables than we need to. I'm devo that you don't know that."

Shepherd looked at me blankly.

"Der, devastated," I said as I walked to the table.

We sat side by side at the table, studying the clues in front of us. I tried not to remember how we had sat like this night after night when we were studying for exams at grad school. Sometimes, completely out of nowhere, he would lean over and give me a kiss, leaving me feeling warm and content.

Closing my eyes, I remembered how my skin tingled at his touch. How his lips felt against mine.

The image of him on that last night flashed through my mind. His eyes glassy and unfocused. His loud voice carrying over those of the other party goers. His erratic movements. My stomach lurched.

Standing up, I stretched and moved myself away from him. I was not going to fall into the trap that was Shepherd. I didn't need to feel that instant disappointment or heartbreak again.

Mantra, come at me – do not get too close, make sure he's not taking drugs.

"Do you want some water?" I asked as I walked into the small, well-appointed kitchen. It had everything we needed, including modern appliances. The bench separated it from the dining/living room. It wasn't huge but it didn't need to be.

Shepherd nodded in response to my water question.

The living room was spacious enough for the two of us. It opened up onto a balcony with a great view of the harbour.

I was grateful that we were in a two-bedroom apartment rather than an open hotel room. I especially liked the fact that we each had a bathroom. It would allow us a degree of separation. I doubt we would continue to stay here though. We were on a budget and something this luxurious wouldn't fit into it.

"Where do you want to start?" Shepherd asked me.

"Usually I'd say to start with the most unique clue in the hope it would lead us to an answer. But none of the clues stand out to me."

He nodded.

I took my time returning to the table where Shepherd was typing a clue into his laptop.

"I've entered the first clue and all that comes up on my search is hurricanes and other random things about people dying."

"Try adding Sydney to the end of the search."

He typed away as I sat beside him. As I leant over to place his glass of water closer to him, the scent I knew as Shepherd hit me — faint musk mixed with his distinct freshness. So masculine, so him. I moved away before it dragged me in. Heat rose in my cheeks and I was grateful that Shepherd was concentrating and hadn't noticed my blush.

"There's a story about bodies being moved for the building of Central Station."

"I'll write that down. Anything else?"

"Nothing that stands out. I'll try the next clue with Sydney on the end, the last place many people saw."

I took a sip of water as I watched Shepherd scroll down through the Google results. I'd missed him terribly when I'd first left the States. He had been a big part of my life for the twelve months I was there. In the first few weeks after I'd left, I'd thought about how much I hadn't told him while we were together. I didn't want to feel the pain anymore. I kept it all inside — my loss, sadness, and guilt. I told him stories of my childhood. The good ones. But didn't tell him how it was all gone. In the end, I thought it was better that I hadn't told him. If I had, I wouldn't have found it so easy to walk away. It was probably flawed logic, but that's what I'd convinced myself of.

"There's nothing here about Central Station. It does talk about Botany Bay, and there are quite a few results about massacres of indigenous people."

"I'll write down Botany Bay."

He didn't type in the next clue but instead clicked on one of the results. As he read, his eyes narrowed and his jaw clenched. I moved closer so I could see what had caused such a reaction. The page spoke about the diseases brought to Australia by the colonists, which wiped out half of the indigenous population of Sydney. Their isolation, although allowing them to live freely for tens of thousands of years, meant they had no immunity. They could not fight off those white man diseases.

But I knew that's not what had affected his mood. The page also spoke about how young indigenous girls and women were sexually abused, and how entire groups of Aboriginals were killed in mass shootings or were driven off cliffs. My stomach dropped as I thought about their fear in their last moments of life before their bodies lay broken and crumpled at the bottom of the cliff.

I tensed. I wanted him to stop reading. Shepherd was a good man. That's why I'd fallen in love with him. It was his reaction to stories like these and the way he wanted to help. He hated knowing people were oppressed or abused and if he continued reading, it would trouble him. I'd read the stories before. I knew how the indigenous were considered subhuman, how some colonists wanted them eradicated, how they laced their food with arsenic. It sickened me. I couldn't do anything about how they were treated in the past. I chose to learn about it, acknowledge it and to do my best to help now, as a lawyer.

I reached over to touch Shepherd's hand on the mouse, trying to distract him, to take his eyes off what he was reading. "Let's go to the next clue."

He read for a moment longer before moving the cursor to

the search bar. "Nothing stands out about grave diggers not keeping detailed records."

"Is there anything that points to Central Station or Botany Bay?"

He scrolled for a couple of pages. From our research during grad school, we knew that sometimes the best information wasn't found on the first page.

"Not that I can see."

He typed in the next clue about unmarked graves on a hillside and I scanned the results with him. There was nothing of significance. Nothing that pointed to the two locations we had already written down. Maybe we were looking at it the wrong way. Sometimes it was not just about what was said, but what was unsaid.

"Let's try looking at the clues another way. If this place was the last place they saw after arriving in Australia, maybe it was also the first."

"OK. If people came to Australia, they were migrants or immigrants. Why don't we search where immigrants or migrants went when they landed in Sydney?"

The results, again, were scattered. They showed us where people went, such as the goldfields or market garden areas, but when we looked at those places with the other clues, nothing matched up.

Shepherd

TARA TOOK her glasses off and rubbed her eyes. We had been sitting and staring at the screen for hours. When I told Sammy to find places for us to hunt and make up the clues, I'd hoped they wouldn't be this difficult. But I guess it wouldn't be worth millions of dollars if it was easy. And the hunt wouldn't take twenty days to complete if we figured out all the clues with hardly any effort. And if the hunt didn't take twenty days, my hope of Tara and I rebuilding our relationship would not likely come to fruition.

Although we had no results, and we were getting nowhere, I enjoyed the time we were spending working together. It felt like old times.

Laying her glasses on the table, Tara stood up and walked to the door leading to the balcony. Her blond hair was tied up in a messy bun. Strands had come loose and settled around her face, brushing her neck, as my lips were begging to do. Her sweat pants hugged her curved butt. I was glad Australian sweatpants were not baggy like ours. The loose t-shirt hid the curves I'd memorised.

"How about we order some lunch?" I suggested, acknowledging my growling stomach.

Tara nodded and grabbed the room service menu off the kitchen bench, scanning it before handing it to me. Glancing at her hands, I noted how her nails were the same as they always had been, cut to a sensible length and unpolished. That was one of the things I was attracted to when we first met, she was real, unpretentious. Five years had passed and it looked like nothing had changed.

"I'll have a burger and chips, please," Tara said.

"Yeah, me too. Mustard and ketchup?"

Giving me a smile, she nodded before turning away and heading for the balcony. I ordered, then joined her out there, taking in the view. I would rather have taken in the view of her, but I didn't think she'd like that.

Yachts were anchored in the cove before us, swaying gently. Their white hulls contrasted the grey water. Bare masts swayed to their own tune. An amusement park stood at the edge of the water, its Ferris wheel turning lazily. Beyond that, the cars on the famous Harbour Bridge moved like ants returning to their colony.

If all of these moving pieces were part of a band, the Ferris wheel would be the bass, slow, low and constant, and the yachts would be the drums, a steady beat. The cars would be the rhythm guitar, constantly changing pace, keeping the song alive.

My gaze drifted to Tara. Standing this close to her made me feel alive. She'd always made me feel this way. When she was with me, I was happy not to be the centre of attention. I only needed to be in her spotlight. I could be myself, not what everyone thought I was. When she left, I became someone different, a party boy with a different girl every other week. But it didn't hold any interest for me. I only did it for something to do. Something to take my mind off her.

After all these years, I still wanted to know why she'd left so suddenly. I never admitted it out loud, but I felt I mustn't have been enough for her. People who love you don't just up and leave without a word.

I would bide my time before asking. But I wouldn't let sleeping dogs lie.

"You still only wear your glasses for reading?" I asked.

"Yeah. You don't wear contacts anymore?"

My heart quickened knowing that she'd noticed. Contacts were another thing I'd dumped along with my party boy ways. "I figured glasses make me look more distinguished."

"They suit you."

The smattering of freckles across her nose and cheeks gave her a youthful look. I wanted to get close to her, to smell her, to see if she still used the same shampoo she had years ago; the one with a hint of vanilla. She was so close to me now, studying my face intently. I wanted to reach out to touch her. I felt the pull towards her, my body moving without my command. My eyes searched hers. My breath faltered as her green eyes gazed at me.

She stepped back, her eyes darted from my face to the view and back to the computer.

"We better keep going."

She walked away.

Tara

SHEPHERD RAN his hand through his hair. It was a classic Shepherd movement when things weren't going to plan.

How often was I going to need to say this bloody mantra – *don't get too close*. Bloody hell, how hard could one simple task be? I didn't even want to be here with him, let alone get close to him. I needed to stop remembering shit about him.

It was late; the sun had set an hour ago. We needed a breakthrough, soon. Nothing we had looked at pointed us to anything helpful. But he kept on going, his concentration didn't waver. He didn't get angry or frustrated—not like a typical drug user.

"Maybe we need to come at this from another angle." He stood up and paced, grabbing a cold chip off his plate as he went. "When pets are brought into Australia, they need to go through quarantine. Maybe at one point people had to do that as well. Maybe it was the first and last place they saw."

"It's worth a try. Type it in."

Shepherd sat next to me again. His eyes went to my lips, and he grinned. He reached out towards me. My heart rate quickened and my skin tingled in anticipation.

"You've got ketchup—" His thumb reached the side of my mouth and wiped across my lips, leaving them heated. It was such a Shepherd thing to do, so natural, I thought nothing of it at first. But we weren't Shepherd and Tara anymore. We were no longer a consist that couldn't be separated, that would be useless apart. We were separated, and for good reason. Just because my lips yearned for his in that moment, it didn't mean I needed to act on it.

"Type it in," I repeated, snatching a serviette off the table. His smile faded as he turned from me.

He typed *quarantine, Sydney*. "Look, there's a quarantine station. For humans."

"Let's type in one of the other clues with that and see what comes up."

How many people died at Q Station?

"This site says 572 died," he said. "That doesn't fit with the clue that no one knows how many died."

"What about this article," I said, pointing down the page of results.

"It says 600, but then goes on to say that records weren't properly documented. That fits with two clues."

Goosebumps rose on my arms. This could be the breakthrough we were waiting for.

"It sure does. And it would have been the first and last place these people saw, if they died there," I said.

"I'll search for unmarked graves on a hillside," he said, opening a new tab, typing quickly. "This article is about an archaeologist searching for unmarked graves at Q Station, and she talks about a cemetery contaminating the water supply."

I reached over and grabbed Shepherd's arm. When he turned to me, I smiled. "We found it. Thank you for not giving up."

"We still make a good team," he said, beaming back at me. My heart fluttered. Damn Shepherd and his effect on me.

I shifted in my seat and looked back at the computer screen.

"The last clue says we can only find it in the dark. They have ghost tours there."

"Looks like we are going on a ghost tour."

***

Shepherd

"I'VE BOOKED us on the tour tomorrow night. It was booked out tonight," I told Tara as she came back into the room.

"OK."

"Do you want to go out and get something to eat?" I was hoping she'd say yes. I wanted to try to build something with her outside of the game. To remind her what we were like before she left.

"Sounds like a good idea. I'm stiff from sitting all day."

We walked into the brisk night air and headed towards

Luna Park. The receptionist had told us there was a nice restaurant just past there on the waterfront. City lights sparkled across the harbour like stars in a dense, dark sky. The glow reflected off the smooth water, giving it a warmth contrary to the brisk air. We were so close to the bridge we could see the linear patterns of light as it rose above us.

We were silent, lost in our own thoughts, the breeze licking at our hair and clothes. I had so many questions I wanted to ask her, but I didn't know where or how to start. We'd never had this problem before. I tried to think of something light to start with.

Two children ran up the walkway towards us, their voices high and their laughter loud. They ran at us so fast I thought we would collide. Their parents called out to them to slow down. But they may as well have been shouting to the moon for all the attention their children paid to them.

Tara and I looked at each other, silently communicating which way we would move. We stepped apart at exactly the same time as the girl turned to check on the boy who was falling behind. She was running backwards, off course, and crashed into Tara. Tara stumbled once, twice and my name escaped her lips, its pitch changing the closer she got to the ground. Her arms flung out trying to grab anything that may break her fall. I reached out to her. In slow motion our hands drifted further and further apart. Instead, I managed to grab hold of the girl's shirt and set her upright. Tara's butt hit the ground and bounced twice before she slid to a stop. A whoosh of air escaped her lips.

Good one Shepherd, save the kid, and let your one and only give a new meaning to gravel rash.

"Are you alright?" I asked the child as her parents ran up

and apologised profusely. The girl was giggling. The boy stood and stared, open-mouthed, at Tara. Tara sat there in the middle of the path and blew strands of hair out of her face. And all I could do was think about how I'd like to ice her butt for her.

Anyone else may have been angry with the child, but Tara laid down in the middle of the track and laughed. She laughed until she cried. The sound of it warmed my heart. This was the Tara I remembered.

The boy continued to stare at her, then turned to his mum and said, "Is she OK, Mummy?"

The mum looked at Tara and back at me before saying, "Did she hit her head?"

"It's OK. She's a bit loopy." I paused and circled my finger around my ear showing just how crazy she was. "I'm just taking her for her nightly walk before I chain her up again."

The boy's eyes grew even wider. "Do you mean like a dog?"

By this time, Tara was crying so hard she was finding it hard to breathe. Her level of crazy went to brand new heights. I bit the inside of my cheek, trying to stop my laugh.

"Will you feed me before you chain me up?" Tara asked sweetly, wiping her tears away and giving me a zany grin.

"Well, OK then, we'll just be leaving you to it," the father said, ushering his family away.

Damn, I loved this woman. Her sense of humour was as whacky as mine.

Our whole relationship had been like this moment... perfect. And then one day she just vanished. Why?

NINETEEN DAYS

Tara

I CHANGED position in the car on the way to Q Station. Every time I moved, I felt the bruises from the night before. Shepherd and I hadn't been able to stop laughing all through dinner. The look on the father's face was priceless. As he ushered his family away the little boy kept looking back, nearly falling over, as he tried to get one last look at the crazy lady still sitting in the middle of the path.

That time together last night was raw. It had been awkward to start with, but after the accident, we'd talked and laughed. I needed to remind myself that I wasn't here to joke with Shepherd or have fun with Shepherd or think about how much I missed him. I was here to win a game. And that three million in prize money would save many lives.

"How cool is this?" Shepherd asked. "I never thought I'd drive over the Sydney Harbour Bridge."

He was right. It was cool. There were six lanes of traffic in the centre, four going one way, two going the other direction, separated by nothing but a white solid line. Then, on the east side, there was a bus lane, a random car lane on its own and a walkway. On the west side, there was a train line and cycleway. It was mind-boggling that something made in 1932 could cater to so much traffic.

We drove between two huge concrete pillars, which towered above us. It was like crossing a threshold into a castle. Then we were underneath the steel arch. It was beautiful, symmetrical, elegant. I stared in wonder at the intricate steelwork. The patterns reminded me of veins on leaves.

"It's amazing," I said, looking over at him.

"It's surprising something so industrial can be so intricate." He used the exact same word I was thinking. We were still so similar even after years apart. Our sense of humour, our thought patterns, our quiet diligence working through the clues. I appreciated that although we felt disappointed and frustrated yesterday when the answers to the clues did not reveal themselves, we never got frustrated with each other.

Our personalities complemented each other and that could help us win the game.

"We're getting close," Shepherd said, breaking into my thoughts.

I shifted in my seat and turned to look out my window. Just because we laughed a little and liked the same things, it didn't mean anything. It certainly didn't mean we were *getting close*. No way. Nah-ah. Nope.

"Q Station here we come. Are you excited?" he asked when I didn't answer.

A bubble of laughter escaped. Q Station was getting close. What was I thinking? "Sure am."

"Me too. This will be our first treasure on the way to six million."

Nineteen more days and I could have three million dollars. Nineteen more days of being with Shepherd. Nineteen more days of maintaining my distance. I could do this.

***

Shepherd

THE TOUR STARTED off benignly enough. We moved through the site in darkness, learning how it operated for over 150 years. Migrants on ships with suspected cases of contagious disease were offloaded and placed into quarantine to protect Sydney's residents.

A few in our tour group carried lanterns to help guide the way. Most lights at the site were turned off to add to the eerie atmosphere.

"The hospital ward is up there, on top of the hill," our tour guide said as we followed her up the winding path. "It's away from the living quarters for isolation purposes."

I looked up ahead of us and back towards the other buildings. It looked like a safe distance apart.

As we climbed the stairs to the ward the guide said, "Many died here from diseases like scarlet fever and Spanish Influenza."

There were two rectangular rooms with basic steel framed beds along each side. Tall French-doors opening onto the balcony separated the beds. When we moved from one room to the other a sudden temperature change occurred. Tara and I stood next to a bed, listening to our guide talk. Before we moved into position, I checked under the bed. I didn't need someone to reach out and grab my leg to scare the crap out of me. It was empty.

We listened to the stories about the nurses who tended to the sick.

Despite the coolness in the room, my left forearm was warm and uncomfortable. Next came pins and needles. A reaction. But to what? I had been wearing the same jacket all evening, so it couldn't be because of that. Maybe something was biting me. I took my jacket off and wiped at my arm. The feeling remained. I shuddered, the hair standing up on the back of my neck.

As soon as the guide stopped talking, I walked back into the other room. I wanted to get outside to have a closer look at my arm in the glow cast from the faint emergency lighting. My arm went back to normal as soon as I crossed the threshold. I shook my head in disbelief.

We walked along the path at the top of the hill, following the guide. She talked about the site of the first cemetery, which lay below us.

"I don't know why they'd bury them on a hill," Tara said. "Didn't they think heavy rains might wash the bodies away?"

"I don't think they were thinking at all, especially seeing that their fresh water source was at the bottom of the hill."

My heart beat faster as we approached the grave diggers' cottage, knowing we were closer to our first treasure. It was a simple weatherboard and corrugated iron building. A door was dead centre with a window placed on each side. The porch was around four feet wide, suffocated by a metre-high banister on two sides. We walked to the far side of the building as the guide climbed the two stairs to the porch. The view overlooked the first grave site.

"They positioned the grave site here, close to the cottage, in case a corpse needed to be buried in the middle of the night," the guide said.

"I guess it was convenient," Tara said to me.

"Yeah, the grave diggers didn't have to go far." I looked around, trying to imagine the site over a hundred years ago; with no lighting, dirt paths, deathly quiet. And then imagined burying bodies in those conditions. I shivered.

Standing outside the cottage the guide faced the group.

"There are a lot of stories about things that went on in this cottage. Stories about drunkenness, torture and death. Creepy Sam, one of the grave diggers, was one of the instigators of much of the madness. We'll hear more about that inside."

Tara gave me a shrug in her no-nonsense way.

"Leave the lanterns on the porch and come into the first room," the guide said as she made her way to the front door. She handed EMF meters out randomly as we entered. One went to Tara. "EMF meters detect changes in frequency, and perhaps, the presence of ghosts. You'll notice as I start talking the EMF lights will respond. They will also change frequency as you move through the cottage."

When we walked into the grave diggers' cottage, Tara and I were separated and stood on opposite sides of the room. The hairs rose on the back of my neck. I searched for her in the darkness of the living room, but with no light the silhouettes were indistinct.

I was in a doorway with my back to the kitchen and the rest of the house. I tensed, not liking being so exposed. It felt like I was being watched from behind. Looking behind me, I saw nothing there. I changed my position so that my back was against the door jamb instead. Taking a deep breath, I tried to listen to our guide as she continued to tell us of the sinister things that reportedly happened in the house.

"The grave diggers loved their rum..."

Movement. In the bedroom. Her voice faded as I peered into the room belonging to Creepy Sam. Shadows played against the wall and window. It was as if someone were moving in there. But how? Everyone was in the small living room. They would have had to walk past me to get there. My eyes were constantly drawn back to the movement as I broke into a cold sweat. The only logical explanation was shadows from the moonlight coming through the open blind.

A shiver rose up my spine. I hoped Tara wasn't freaked out like me. All I wanted was to be near her, to feel safe with her.

"One night there was a party. Some of the ladies who worked in the dining hall were present..." The guide's tone was ominous, I looked again to the bedroom. When I was not distracted by the shadows, I was searching Tara out. Where was she? I couldn't distinguish her from the other silhouettes in the crowd. I needed to move. I shifted my weight from foot to foot.

The guide finished her startling exposé, not that I'd heard much. The group split up. Some went to the bedroom at the front of the house. Others passed me and made their way through the house while I waited for Tara to join me. We walked into Creepy Sam's bedroom together. The blind was closed. That was weird. If the blind was closed, where did the shadows come from?

"Did you close the blind?" I asked the guide.

"No. It's always been closed."

My stomach clenched.

"Are you sure?"

Tara

I WATCHED SHEPHERD CLOSELY. It was unusual for him to disbelieve someone and question them twice. It would be different in a court room but not here.

"What's going on, Shep?"

"I saw shadows in this room, moving, sort of like a person rocking back and forth. I thought it was light and shadow from the open blind."

As soon as he finished talking the EMF in my hand started lighting up. My heart rate picked up in response. I wanted to hand the EMF off to someone, but there was no one to give it to but the guide, and she resisted. I looked back at Shepherd. He was still in the same spot, next to the wardrobe. Without warning the wardrobe door swung open.

"Um—," was all I managed before the door smacked into his arm. My heart thumped in my chest as I watched his eyes open wide. He took hold of the door and stepped in front of the wardrobe. As I held my breath he looked inside. I knew sceptical, sensible Shepherd was looking for a mechanism that would have caused the door to open on its own. He shook his head and closed it firmly.

A thought entered my mind out of nowhere: *Creepy Sam sometimes hid inside the wardrobe.* I shook my head. Why would I think that? Creepy Sam was the instigator of much of the evil, not the victim. I moved to exit the room, and Shepherd looked ready to follow. The wardrobe door swung open again and banged into his arm. Shepherd froze as I nearly jumped out of my skin, and I practically threw the EMF at the guide as I grabbed Shepherd's hand and pulled him out of the room.

"Let's just find what we are here to find and get out of this place," I said, still gripping his hand tightly.

We walked to the back of the cottage where the bathroom was. I scanned the area, looking for something out of the ordinary, an item that didn't seem to belong. In the corner behind a random wooden chair, something glowed faintly. I made my way towards it. Still freaking out from what happened in Creepy Sam's room, my hand shook as I reached for it. It was a coin. One side had my initials, the other side Shepherd's. Shepherd smiled as I showed him, before I put it in my pocket and followed him out.

Our last stop was the shower block. I'd had enough excitement for one evening and would gladly have missed it, but our guide insisted the group go in together. There was a central corridor stretching before us, housing cubicle after cubicle. There were two outer corridors as well, along the outer walls. All in all, there were at least eighty shower stalls.

"When ships docked, the first thing the passengers had to do was come in here to shower."

I looked around imagining those passengers' thoughts at such an inhumane building.

"The shower water contained carbolic acid, to wash disease away. After a few days, their skin would peel off."

"Welcome to Australia," I said, shaking my head.

Corrugated iron walls, open doorways and cold, inhumane concrete floors were all we could see. The passengers stepped down into the shower so that its water was contained and did not flow into other cubicles.

I had no hesitation keeping hold of Shepherd's hand. Having him close gave me comfort. As we walked past the gaping doorways, I couldn't get to the end fast enough. Adrenalin spurred me on. As soon as we hit the end of the corridor, we chose the left path. When we got to the next corner, a chill ran up my spine. I gripped Shepherd's hand tighter. We looked at each other, said 'fuck no', and abruptly turned the other way.

We walked down the other corridor instead, keeping ourselves as close to the outside wall as we could. As we passed each shower cubicle, we glanced inside. Within one stood a solid black figure. My heart nearly stopped; I yelped and Shepherd swore. Clutching each other, we sped up, while my heart raced, until we were free from the overwhelming dread.

Shepherd

"WELL, that was something new for us," I said as I unlocked the door to our room.

Tara nodded. "Probably not something we need to experience again."

"Yeah. I'd rather not."

Tara was within arm's length. My heart rate quickened as my eyes followed the flow of her hair across her breasts. The blond in direct contrast to her navy cotton shirt. My hands longed to touch her in more ways than one.

Tara took a step back and my eyes were drawn back to her face.

"Goodnight, Shepherd."

"Goodnight."

I watched her walk to her room, wishing I could follow. But even if she wanted me to, I couldn't. I needed to make some calls. I needed to find people to invest $3 million into her foundation. I had a lot of connections and knew a lot of rich people; family, friends, clients. I would just need to persuade them. Or, more likely, Sammy would need to persuade them. I couldn't very well make phone call after phone call without being caught, and I didn't want Tara to find out it was just a game I made up to win her back. Not yet, anyway. Would she forgive me? Maybe there'd be a chance if I managed to raise the funds for her.

I called Sammy as I closed my bedroom door behind me. Two doors and the living room between us would block my voice from Tara.

"Hi, Shepherd, how is operation 'win back Tara' going?"

"We've stumbled onto a bit of a problem." I kept my voice low.

"What, you realised this was a stupid idea?"

"No, the idea is solid. We are getting along well."

"But she hasn't fallen into your arms yet declaring her love for you?" There was laughter in his voice. "Or you've realised that this whole thing edges on the verge of being creepy?"

"Well, maybe a little."

"I still don't know why you just couldn't call her."

"Some things are done better in person."

"Yeah, like stalking." Sammy laughed like it was one of the funniest things he'd heard.

"Sammy, shut up and listen." The firmness in my voice had the desired effect. "She has plans for the money. She wants to set up a foundation in her brother's name."

"Shit! If this were real, there would be no guarantee that you would win."

"I know that. But she isn't going to see it that way. She will never forgive me."

"Maybe you'd be surprised. She may be impressed with how much effort you went to." His voice was calm. I wish my anxiety would respond to it.

I sank onto the bed and ran my hand through my hair. "The first thing she said when she saw me was, 'You've got to be fucking kidding me.' I don't think she'll be that forgiving."

"Shit, Shep, how are we going to come up with three million? How much do you have in your trust fund?'

"Three hundred thousand. And I don't get another payment until next year. We can use all of what I have."

"I can probably put in a hundred thousand."

"Thanks, Sammy."

I didn't even have to ask. If the situation were reversed, I would have done exactly the same for him. We'd been friends for as long as my memory stretched back. Maybe it was inevitable, seeing that our fathers had been childhood friends. My father had backed Sammy's dad in his early political career and still did. When the time came, and I'm sure it would, where Sammy would take over the reins, I would be there for him in exactly the same way.

I held my head in my hands. Nineteen days left. How

could we possibly pull this off? I was glad I'd added that rule about having to stay together for the whole twenty days. When I made it up, it was so Tara and I would have enough time to rekindle what we had. Now, it would give Sammy and I extra time to raise the money.

What if we did all this and found out there was no future for Tara and me? I shook my head. That wasn't the point. This was my chance to do something to help her help the people she thought were important.

"With Tara's entry fee, that leaves $2.4 million," Sammy said.

"Can you start doing some ringing around please? I can text you a bunch of names. I'd do it myself but those rules I made up make it somewhat difficult."

"What can I tell them about this foundation?"

I gave him all the details I had. Lucky Sammy was the influential type. He'd worked on his dad's campaigns and brought in a lot of money. And if he could set it up so that they could use it as a tax deduction, they might be more willing to donate.

"Give me a few days."

"Thanks, Sammy. I owe you one."

"Maybe you'll listen to me next time when I say something is a bad idea."

"Yeah. Maybe."

He laughed. We both knew that wasn't likely.

"How is she?" Sammy asked.

"Just the same as always. Beautiful. Driven. Perfect."

"Oh man, you've got it bad."

I imagined him rolling his eyes.

"Yep." I thought about Tara's lips, how I wanted to kiss

her, to drive my tongue into her mouth. And other places. Crap, I had a hard on. And I shouldn't have one of those while speaking to my best friend.

"Has she said why she left?"

"Not yet."

"You know you can't fix anything until it's out in the open? *Everything*. Why she left and what effect it had on you."

"I know." I did know. But it was too soon to ask her. I needed her to feel comfortable with me before I broached that subject. We had moments where I felt we were connecting but not enough yet. "I want to tell her what happened when she left but I don't want her thinking me going off the rails was her fault."

"No, your behaviour wasn't her fault. But she needs to understand what happened and what her part in that was." He sighed. "Call me in a few days. I'll let you know how I'm going raising the funds. How did the first hunt go?"

"That was some freakish shit." I told Sammy about the hunt, shuddering while thinking about Creepy Sam. The weirdness that my best friend and that creepy dude had the same name was not lost on me.

I deleted the call log as soon as I hung up. Sammy was right about me calling her. It all seems so irrational now. But I was scared she wouldn't listen. When she left, I tried contacting her any way I could think of, but she ignored each attempt. I thought seeing her in person would mean she couldn't ignore me. Stupid.

EIGHTEEN DAYS

Tara

THE SUNLIGHT FILTERED into the room through a gap in the curtains. I watched dust particles dancing in the stream of light.

Two days ago, I wondered how I would be able to work with Shepherd. I needn't have worried. It was much too easy. Sitting side by side, working on the clues together, felt like old times. The way we held hands at Q Station, the familiarity of his touch and the comfort it gave me. Yep, all too easy.

But I needed to focus on winning. The stats always consumed me. Twenty-eight percent of young people experiment with illicit drugs. One in five deaths are drug related. Foster children, youth with mental health, Indigenous youth and LBGTQ+ youth are more likely to have substance abuse disorders than their counterparts. Up to five times more likely in some cases. These people are the most vulnerable. They needed help. Zachariah didn't fit into any of these categories. Yet, he'd needed help. Help I couldn't give.

So, as much as I wanted to stay away from Shepherd, I couldn't. The chance of winning three million outweighed my wants. How much I once loved him did not matter. I couldn't afford to think about it. And I needed to rein in any residual feelings...for eighteen more days.

After showering, I went out to the living area. Shepherd was on the balcony reading a book. A man reading a book was undeniably attractive. Shepherd reading a book, with his messy hair and small smile at whatever held his attention, was even more so. He looked up and smiled at me; I returned one automatically, failing to ignore the warmth spreading through me. So much for my resolve. I needed to get a grip.

"Do you want some breakfast?" he asked, as I sat in the chair beside him.

"Yes, I'm starving."

"We can order room service."

"OK. But our budget is pretty tight. We can't keep having room service."

"Lucky we have a kitchen. I spoke to the manager earlier. She said they're not heavily booked, so we agreed we could have the apartment for $180 a night. With the hire car costing $400, we still have $1000 to spend."

Shepherd was not usually the type to wheel and deal. He happily paid full price. He believed the fees went to keeping people employed and paid fairly. But he was always conscious of where he spent his money. If we went out for lunch, he would try to find a place with sustainable practices or that would give a free meal to someone for each one we bought. If we stayed somewhere, it would always be somewhere nice, but without an exorbitant price tag. He had nothing to prove. Another thing that made me fall deeper in love with him. And another thing I needed to push out of my mind.

I needed to remember why we weren't a good match. Recalling how I felt when I saw him at his share house, and how he hadn't even noticed me standing there watching him. That's what I needed to feel to bring me out of my fantasy land.

Studying him closely, I said, "You're taking this seriously."

He gave a small shrug. "No point failing because we can't stick to a budget. You've told me how important this is to you."

I nodded, happy he wasn't just treating it like a game.

"Have we received the next set of clues?" We'd sent the photo of our find last night once we got back to the car. If time was of the essence, we didn't want to linger.

"Not exactly." He handed me the phone.

I was expecting the next set of clues; instead, we'd received a reminder about the rules. It's not like I had forgotten them. Especially the first one — we must stay together at *all* times.

"Did you speak to the manager in person?'

"Yes."

My stomach sank.

"Do you think leaving the room would break the rules? Will we get penalised for that?"

<hr>

Shepherd

TARA'S EYES widened as she asked the question. They were unflinching as she waited for my answer.

"I didn't leave the room. I asked her to come up here. I didn't want to risk it," I said. The truth was, I had thought about going down to see her but was worried that Tara might wake up and find me gone. The rules were fake, just like the whole game, but Tara didn't know that.

After I had spoken to Sammy last night I lay in bed and thought about the predicament I'd gotten myself into. In the end, I'd convinced myself that nothing had changed. The plan had never been to tell her the truth about the game early on. I needed to stick to that plan, so I had a chance to raise the money for the prize. And to win Tara over.

Then my thoughts turned to her and how good she looked. How good her hand felt in mine. The warmth we shared when we stood close to each other. I thought about all the things I wanted to do with her. About how good she would taste on my tongue. My dick was hard and there was no relief in sight. My only solace would be her.

Sammy was right, I did have it bad. And I didn't know if that would lead to the love of my life coming back to me or a heartbreak that would end any chance of a future together.

Tara's face softened and her shoulders relaxed. "That was a good idea."

"I'm getting bacon and eggs for breakfast; do you want the same?'

"No, I don't think they'll make them as good as you do. I'll have pancakes."

I smiled at her remark. I'd made breakfast for us whenever we spent the night together. She always thanked me and told me how fluffy my eggs were and how juicy the bacon was and how I had timed the toast just right, so it was still warm when served. And it was the best bacon and eggs she'd ever had.

The way she complimented me felt good. It felt good then. It felt good now.

That simple remark felt like a win. A move away from possible heartbreak.

Her responding smile wavered and her mouth turned down into a frown. "Shepherd, I think we need to set some ground rules about us and this competition."

The use of my full name was a stab to my heart. Swallowing hard, I fought to keep the disappointment off my face. I waited for her to continue.

***

Tara

"I ENJOY SPENDING time with you. I always have. But I'm here for the game and the game alone. We need to keep our focus on the job at hand and our communication should revolve solely around the hunt."

I had so much more to say but it all sounded childish and petty. It was like I was accusing him of not being able to control himself. But this was more my problem than it was his. I was the one feeling the warm, fuzzy feelings. I could tell him we shouldn't cook together, eat together or drink together. How stupid would that be? We would be living together; it wasn't unreasonable to think we'd eat together. So, before I set any more ground rules, I talked myself out of it.

He smiled, his lips tight and his eyes assuming the vacant look that meant he was thinking. "And food. Our conversation needs to revolve around that, too."

His tone was so matter of fact it made me smile—inwardly. I made sure it was only inwardly.

He didn't protest any of my ground rules, not that there were many. And by many, I meant one, only communicate about the game. Maybe I was reading too much into it. Maybe he was just here for the game as well. Although, he never said he was. Actually, he had never said why he was here, what his motive or reason was for joining the game.

"Why are you here, Shepherd?"

His brow furrowed. "Because we've been teamed up in a scavenger hunt?"

Ugh. As a lawyer, I should know not to ask such an ambiguous question. "Why did you join the hunt?"

"I remembered how much fun you said they were."

What else did he remember about me? About us? I remembered enough for both of us. I blushed, turned away, and let it drop.

As we were eating breakfast, our phones vibrated—the next clues. Shepherd read over them and his brow furrowed. He handed the phone to me. Just like the last set of clues, they gave nothing away.

Hunt 2
**We have one of the best views in
    Sydney.**
**We were first established in the
    1800s.**
**Science is our thing. In fact, we like
    to science the shit out of things.**
Colour is always a delight.

Your treasure will be found in one of the four elements, geometrically shaped.

Again, none of the clues stood out. I handed the phone back to Shepherd. He wrote the clues down and looked over to me. "Same process as last time?"

"I think so."

"The clues aren't easy. No wonder they've given us twenty days to complete the hunt."

Until then, I had forgotten that even if we finished the hunt early, we would still need to stay together for the full twenty days. Oh well, it would be worth it if we won the six million.

"How many places have views that are bonza?" I asked.

Shepherd gave me a sideways glance.

"Too many," was his simple response as he scrolled through the Google results.

"Deadset?"

"What?"

This was too much fun. "Deadset?"

"What are you even talking about?" He rolled his eyes.

I struggled to keep my laughter in. "*Deadset* means 'is that true?'"

He sighed. "I think we should be able to narrow some down with the second clue. Not many could have been established in the 1800s."

"OK. Let's write a list of the places with the best views and go through them one by one."

He read out the names and I wrote them down. There were quite a few places claiming to have the best views. And from some of the pictures they shared, they had the right to make that claim—sweeping views of the harbour with the Bridge, the Opera House, the ocean, the city. We wrote at least forty names down and were able to eliminate the more modern ones straight away, like the Icebergs at Bondi and the Blue Mountains Botanic Garden, because they opened in the 1900s.

In a way, I was glad it was Shepherd I was paired with, out of all the people on the hunt. After all this time, we still worked well together. He was hardworking, and I knew he wouldn't slack off. Having known each other prior meant we didn't need to get to learn about each other first, which was a huge bonus. Although a lot felt familiar, some things didn't. Like the awkwardness I sometimes felt around him. That had never existed before.

At first, after I'd left, I had searched for him online to see what he was up to. Scrolling through his Facebook, I hadn't been impressed. He was tagged in photos with girls and always seemed to be partying. I'd tortured myself for a few months and then stopped looking. I was sad that he had moved on so quickly. Maybe even angry. But I was happy I was out. It was a scene I didn't want to be in.

Every now and then though, I would feel the inclination to type his name in a search bar. I don't know why. Maybe it was curiosity. Maybe I missed him. Maybe I was lonely. When I searched, the party boy photos had disappeared. He'd made the paper a few times for his work with immigrants.

Was he still working with immigrants now? What else was he doing? Was he seeing someone? I had seen no photos of him with a partner. If he was seeing someone, I don't know how I'd handle it. But I had no right to feel that way or begrudge him happiness. I was the one who'd left him.

I refrained from asking him any questions. I did not want him to think I held an interest in him outside of the hunt. Even if I did. What was wrong with me? I did not have feelings for Shepherd Bell III. And even if I did, there was no future for us. I was better off alone, where heartbreak could not hurt me.

"Do you want to take a break? I'm stiff from sitting for so long," he said, stretching his back,

"Good idea. I could do with something to eat."

Shepherd smiled. "You always snacked when we studied. Nothing much has changed with you."

We knew each other so well once. I didn't want him to think he still did. I didn't know why. I didn't even want to admit it to myself. "Plenty has changed with me."

His smile turned into a hard line.

Shepherd

HER COMMENT WAS firm and final, but I didn't want the conversation to stop. I wanted to know more about her, about what she had been doing over the last five years. To be honest, I knew about most of it already. I always searched for her online, even when I was trying to mend my broken heart by partying. I listened as mutual friends spoke about her; about the amazing things she was doing. It was tragic, really, how I searched out news of her.

She'd joined the UN six months after she left, working in

Africa and the Middle East before returning to Australia. I don't know exactly what she did in the UN. I do know she met a doctor who she'd had a relationship with. I was devastated she had found someone to share her dream with that wasn't me. I don't know why I tortured myself looking for her. I'm not ashamed to admit I was happy when I'd heard they'd broken up.

She had followed her dream, and I'd done nothing except fall back into the life expected of me – working for my father in his law firm. There was nothing wrong with the law he practiced. It wasn't immoral. His clients were mainly corporate. But I wanted to help *real* people with *real* problems. My father could see I wasn't happy and didn't stop me from running free clinics. It wasn't the same as what Tara had done, though.

I wanted to ask her about it, about her life then and now. But she was clear before about wanting to communicate about the hunt only. The closest personal thing I could ask about was the foundation. The one in memory of her brother.

"Tell me about your foundation," I said as I closed the door behind us.

"I'm in the process of setting it up. I thought about setting up an office in the city, but decided that may not be accessible enough for the people I want to help."

"That's how you came up with the idea of an outreach van?"

"Yes. We would have a counsellor who travels in the van. If they encounter people who require legal assistance, I would join them on their next trip."

I nodded, wondering who *we* was, but I was too afraid to ask. I waited for her to continue as we entered the lift.

"For safety reasons, the counsellor will have one or two others with them at all times. In case they face volatile situations."

"That's a good idea."

We stood side by side against the back wall, almost touching. So close, I could feel her warmth. I forced the hand closest to her to rest against my leg. Its natural inclination was to reach for hers. I was sure if that happened, she would retreat from me further.

"When I was in the UN we weren't allowed to travel alone. We had local escorts."

She was talking. I needed to keep that going.

"Were they armed?"

"Generally, not. It had to be an exceptional circumstance to use an armed escort. There is a list of criteria to be met."

I had worried about her then. I still worried about her. But I couldn't tell her that. She wasn't ready to hear it. Whatever made her leave me still held firm. I needed to figure out what it was so I could convince her that it was no longer an issue.

The lift door opened, and we walked out into the bright lobby. Again, I was painfully aware of her hand hovering close to mine. Before my hand even moved, she jerked away from me, almost like we were opposite poles on a magnet and she was being repelled.

She stopped in the middle of the lobby to pat a small dog. I didn't realise it was a pet friendly hotel. I guess the photos of pets on the wall should have given it away but when I'd arrived, I had been so nervous about meeting her, I hadn't noticed. She stood up and made her way to the reception desk. Not even acknowledging me. Our discussion was over. For now.

"Is there a supermarket or grocery store close by?" she asked the male receptionist.

"Just a few blocks that way." He indicated towards the left.

Catching up to her as she walked out the doors, I fell into line beside her. "So, these extra people you have in the van, will they be security guards?"

"No, I want them to be people we've helped. People who feel like they have nothing to contribute. I want them to see they matter, that they have something to give."

"And who are you going to try to help first?"

She didn't look at me as she answered, not even as we stood at the traffic lights. "I would like to start with those at risk of substance abuse. They don't need to be those I mentioned, like kids in foster care or LBGQT. We will help anyone."

We passed old buildings mixed in with the new, the path beside them narrowing in parts. Traffic was hectic even though it was the middle of the day. Noise was our constant companion.

"How will you know who to help?"

"We won't force ourselves on anyone. We will establish ourselves in certain areas and let them come to us. Others will be referred by community workers, homeless shelters, churches, anyone really."

That was a good strategy.

"Is this tactic something you learnt in the UN? Getting people to come to you?"

"Yes. I found that when one person was brave enough to approach us, the community watched what happened. They gained knowledge and trust from observing and then approached us themselves."

"How would you help them?"

The harshness in her voice dissipated. She turned to me as she spoke. "After we built rapport, we explained to them how we were there to help and what the mobile court was there to do. They would slowly open up to us. It was a slow, difficult process; trust takes time. We had successful convictions for violence and sexual violence."

"So, the plan is to help the vulnerable in a different way now, in memory of your brother?'

"Yes."

"Was he part of the vulnerable groups you mentioned before?"

"No."

She picked up her pace unexpectedly. I jogged to catch up to her.

"But he died from drug abuse?"

Tara

IT WAS inevitable that we'd talk about Zac. That's why I was here, after all. Shepherd and I had been together for twelve months and I'd never spoken a word to him about Zac dying. I wanted to protect myself from the pain. And when I'd found Shepherd high, I knew not telling him was the right thing to do. I didn't need him to know my pain and then throw it in my face.

Yet Shepherd seemed perfectly normal now. His eyes

weren't erratic, glassy or lost. He wasn't jumping out of his skin or at the other end of the spectrum, totally exhausted. He was able to concentrate and make clear, rational decisions. The signs weren't there.

I needed to tell him *something*. I needed him to know why the foundation was important to me. Why this competition was important to me.

"Yes. Zac died from an overdose."

I left my explanation at that. The pain was still raw after all these years.

"I couldn't help Zac, but maybe I can help someone else."

Shepherd grabbed my hand and gave it a squeeze before letting it go again. Reassuring me with that tiny gesture...more than it should have.

"You'll get the money, Tara. We can do this."

I nodded.

Walking into the supermarket, Shepherd grabbed a basket and we made our way down the aisles.

"Do you want bacon and eggs for breakfast?' Shepherd asked.

"Are you cooking?"

"Do you think you can make better scrambled eggs than me?" He gave me a sly grin.

"I may have learnt some new skills over the past five years."

Was I trying to remind him of the time we'd spent apart? Or was I trying to remind myself that we'd grown apart?

"So, you're cooking breakfast then?" he asked, his eyebrow cocked.

"No, bacon and eggs are your speciality. Let's see if

they're as good as I remember them." I gave him a small nudge, smiling.

"They may be even better."

"I doubt that."

I left him there, standing at the eggs while I disappeared down another aisle. I needed some distance. I needed to remember to be angry with him. It was his actions, his stupidity, that had driven me away.

We couldn't buy too much, as we didn't know what the organisers had in store for us. We might need to leave Sydney and we couldn't very well lug days' worth of food with us. I grabbed a loaf of wholemeal bread. Before I met Shepherd, I was a white bread girl. That's what we always had on the farm. Sometimes my grandmother would make it from scratch. The smell of bread filtered through the house, making our mouths water. As soon as it came out of the oven, the four of us would sit down and devour a whole loaf. She learnt soon after we moved in with them, she would need to make two loaves if she actually wanted to use it for sandwiches or toast. I placed the loaf in the basket when Shepherd caught up.

"What do you want on your sandwiches?" I asked.

"Do you still like ham, cheese and tomato?"

"Yes." Maybe I hadn't changed that much.

"Let's go with that then."

I spotted some bags of chips at the end of the aisle, grabbed a couple and threw them towards Shepherd. He caught them expertly with the basket. His smile nearly stopped me in my spot. That smile haunted me while I dated Emilio, a doctor I was with in the UN. I always felt like I was cheating on Emilio with Shepherd, just through thought alone. That's why I broke up with him. It wasn't fair to him.

He was kind and thoughtful and he deserved someone who was devoted to him, not someone devoted to someone she could never have.

I threw a bag of lollies into the basket.

"If you keep throwing junk in there, we'll end up the size of a house," Shepherd said with a deep chuckle.

"It's OK. I'll still love you." It came out without my even thinking about it. I dropped my gaze and turned with my heart in my throat. This was bad. I did not still love Shepherd.

"Tacos for dinner?" he asked, glossing over my comment. Why did he have to be everything good, just like I remembered?

"Sounds good."

It looked like Shepherd was doing all the cooking tonight. I didn't mind. His childhood housekeeper, Maria had taught him well. He always added a good amount of spice to give it some kick.

***

Shepherd

WE WALKED BACK to the apartment in silence. I thought about what Tara had said about her brother. He must have died just before she came to the States for grad school. I knew they went to uni together. She had never even come close to mentioning his death to me. The way she spoke, I always thought he was still alive in Australia.

How had her parents coped with losing their son and then having their daughter move across the world for a year? After that, she'd joined the UN, which I wouldn't consider the safest job in the world. They must have been stressed. But if they were anything like her, they would be encouraging, loving, and would not hold her back.

She hadn't talked about her parents much. But I had known that she always called home once a week. Always Sunday evening, Australian time. She always said that time suited them best. She never once complained about getting up at 3am to call, and it didn't matter where we were, she never missed it.

We ate lunch as we sat back down at our computer and went through our list.

"How many 'best views' are we left with?" Tara asked.

"We've still got eight."

"That's more than I thought. We'll have to go through them one by one with the other clues."

"'Science is our thing and colour is always a delight.'"

"Let's start with the Manly Ferry, which started operations in the 1850s. It travels the harbour for eighteen hours a day, so the views are certainly good. I guess you could say it's colourful with all the different people using it. But it doesn't relate to science."

I struck it off the list before starting on the next one. "Mrs Macquarie's Chair. That was built in 1810. I don't think you could get much of a better view. It overlooks the harbour near the Sydney Harbour Bridge and the Opera House. But there's nothing colourful about a chair of sandstone."

"No, and there's nothing scientific about it either."

I struck it off the list.

"George's Heights lookout. That's in the same position as the chair, not scientific or colourful."

"Circular Quay, Fort Denison and Cockatoo Island

would be the same," I said, crossing them out. This hunt was progressing much better than the first. We weren't scrambling for an answer.

"Which leaves us with the Royal Botanic Garden, which opened in 1816, and the Sydney Observatory, built in 1857," Tara said, tapping each of the uncrossed names on the notepad.

"Well, I imagine the gardens are colourful. Stars and planets not so much." I ran my hand through my hair.

"Yes, but the observatory definitely covers the science aspect of the clues. Do the gardens?"

"Let's look at their website."

Tara's eyes widened as I clicked onto the website and we found a whole section on the home page dedicated to science. "Wait, what about the other part of the clue 'science the shit out of things'?"

"It sounds familiar. Like something I've heard before. Let's look it up."

"Look, it was a movie quote," Tara said, excitedly.

"Yeah, I remember that movie. It was *The Martian* and Matt Damon was an astronaut stuck on Mars."

"Was he a scientist?"

I hit a link. "He was a botanist."

"I think this is it. We need to find the treasure in the gardens."

I leant over and gave her a kiss, a quick peck on the lips, which she reciprocated. A flush rose on my face. And it was not the only thing blood rushed to. Tara snapped her head back to the screen.

Breathe. Just breathe. I needed to slow down my jittery heart. I was in this for the long game. I had to control myself, as hard as that might be when all I wanted to do was take her in my arms and claim her lips.

"The last clue says it will be in one of the four elements, geometrically shaped – earth, air, fire and water," I said.

"It's not likely to be air or fire, so that leaves earth and water."

"How can they be geometrically shaped?" I leant back in my chair and rubbed the back of my neck, thinking about geometric shapes. Tara moved the laptop towards her and scrolled through pictures of the gardens.

"I don't know. If it's water...maybe it's a pond or a fountain."

"Maybe. What are their opening hours?" I asked her.

"They close at six."

"We don't have time to go today." It disappointed me we couldn't go immediately. It had taken us all afternoon to learn about those last few places. But we had twenty days, in total. It looked like Sammy planned it out so we would use every one of them.

"I guess we will need to wait until tomorrow then. We can head there straight after breakfast. I don't want to lose time or risk falling behind," she said, closing the laptop.

Tara

SHEPHERD and I sat on the couch side by side and watched *The Martian* while we ate dinner. The warmth from where our arms touched seeped through me. I should have moved away, but I didn't want to. The spices from the tacos radiated off him. What would they taste like when mixed with the sweetness of him? My eyes were drawn to his lips, the curve of them. I could practically feel their softness.

Shepherd turned his face to mine. My eyes lingered for a moment as I imagined his soft breath brushing my face as he bent his head toward me. My breathing shallowed to the point that it was nearly non-existent, as if I were a starfish. I turned my face away and resumed watching the movie, making sure my hands kept to themselves and my thoughts remained on the man saving his own life on the screen. Matt Damon may have been the most attractive astronaut I'd ever seen, but he was nothing compared to Shepherd.

The movie ended and I sat there while the credits rolled. Our closeness suddenly made me feel like we were in a flux capacitor. Time—five years of it—had been starved, and now it was swallowing me whole. Everything about Shepherd felt like home. Everything. And if I allowed it to, this feeling wouldn't just swallow me, it would become me.

I jerked away from him, my heart racing, my skin cold, while I broke into a sweat. I couldn't allow this to happen. Shepherd was no longer my solace. He never truly was because he never knew my grief. My grief over my brother. The feelings of loss at my parent's death.

No, Shepherd was not my solace. Not then. Not now.

Standing, I didn't look at him. Instead, I said a quiet goodnight before walking to my bedroom. I sat on my bed and stared at the wall.

Shepherd

AFTER TARA WENT to her room, I sat and stared at the blank TV screen. Sometimes I felt like things were falling into place. The way she looked at me during the movie, how her eyes were drawn to me, my lips, is precisely how she used to be. When my face turned towards hers my heart was racing, like I'd just finished a hill climb. I wanted to take her face, to feel how it was made to fit in my hands. I wanted to embrace her lips with mine, to capture them and remind them they belonged to me alone. I wanted to show her I was hers, one body part at a time.

As if she had awoken from a spell, she had turned her face away from mine and hadn't acknowledged my presence once after that. When we reached the bittersweet part of the movie her hand did not hold mine like it once would have.

Eighteen days, soon to be seventeen, was all I had left to make us Shepherd and Tara again. Eighteen days to find $3 million. I didn't know which goal, if any, was more achievable.

Sitting forward, I rested my elbows on my knees and my head in my hands. How would I break through this wall she created? What had caused her to become so estranged? What had I done and how could I undo it? One thing was for sure, I needed to raise this money for her foundation, for her brother or else I would never have a chance to repair what we'd lost. Three million dollars was a huge amount. Two point four million was a huge amount.

I went to the table and turned on the laptop. Opening a new window, I logged into my email and scanned my inbox. There was nothing from Sammy. I sent him a short note asking for an update on what he'd raised. I would check again tomorrow.

As I was clicking the red x to close the window Tara came out of her room. My head jolted in her direction. Her movements were stiff as she walked towards me with narrowed eyes. My heart raced. I was grateful that the tingling on my skin was only evident to me.

"What are you doing?"

"Just thought I'd try to figure out a game plan for tomorrow."

She stopped beside me; her arms crossed over her chest. I'd never lied to her before. I had no idea if I was convincing or not. I knew how to bluff as good as any lawyer, but that was in a courtroom or against an opposition while negotiating. This was not the same. This was someone I loved. My heart thumped. It surprised me it couldn't be seen through my t-shirt.

"What have you come up with?"

Damn, think quick Shepherd.

"We will need to get a map."

Yeah, because that idea was so enlightening. She continued to look at me. I could think quick in front of the most horrendous people when questioning them on the stand, but right now my brain had left me completely. I took in a breath and smiled, stalling for time, letting oxygen infiltrate my brain to get the thinking juices flowing. The pause felt like a lifetime but lasted two seconds maximum. Still too long, but it was the best I could do.

I must have looked like an idiot.

"Then we could ask a guide to mark all the fountains and ponds. It would save us time."

She nodded. "That's a good idea. The rules said we could ask for help once we arrived at our destination."

My heart slowed. I kept my position. I didn't want her to see my body relax, as it may raise suspicion.

"I'm going to bed now. Goodnight, Tara."

"Goodnight."

Walking to my room, I listened as she walked to the sink and turned on the tap to fill a glass of water.

Idiot. I needed to be more careful.

SEVENTEEN DAYS

Tara

I TOOK in the view as we crossed Sydney Harbour on the ferry. It was surreal being so close to the Sydney Harbour Bridge, an iconic landmark that people around the world recognised. Seeing it from a different angle, from the water, only increased its dreamlike, unique quality. Steel beams formed linear patterns, vertical, horizontal and diagonal, so elaborate it was a piece of art. The steel arch rose into the sky, reminding me of a caterpillar arching its back, its delicate patterns perfectly symmetrical.

As we walked through the gates of the botanical gardens, the steel columns towering up beside us were eternal guards at the entrance of a wonderland, the electricity between us was almost palpable. I was so charged that as Shepherd reached for my hand, I didn't withdraw. It was like the magnetic power of the universe was drawing our hands together and there was nothing I could do to stop it. The current intensified almost to the point that if we let go of each other we would be suspended in nothingness, becoming immobile.

So much for rules. I couldn't even keep the single one I had created. And that was about talking. Physical contact was a whole new level. I was so weak where Shepherd was concerned. And even as I berated myself, I still held his hand. What the hell?

Hand in hand we walked to reception and asked for a map.

"We are completing a scavenger hunt. We think one of our treasures is hiding in the garden. Could you please mark where the water features are?" Shepherd asked.

"A scavenger hunt sounds like fun. There are quite a few water features," the guide said, considering the map.

"What about ones that are geometrically shaped?" I suggested.

"That narrows it down." She circled the water features on the map.

"Thanks," Shepherd said as he took the marked map. Then, looking between me and the map, he asked, "Where do you want to start?"

"Maybe we should try the other entrance fountain and work our way in."

"I would suggest you visit The Calyx first as it's on the way to the Morstead Fountain," the helpful guide suggested.

"Sounds like a plan. Thanks."

Shepherd did not let go of my hand as we followed the path through lush green manicured lawns. We stopped at the Lewis Wolfe Levy Fountain, made of grey and red granite. The sides were scalloped, so it was not on our list, but we couldn't help but examine it anyway. In the middle, on a high block, stood a bronze statue of a woman surrounded by a heron and reeds. The sound of the running water helped regulate my heart rate. On the four corners were bubblers shaped like a vintage champagne glass. We separated to climb the steps to look into each bubbler but no treasure was to be found.

"It's so peaceful here," I said, looking around. There wasn't another soul in sight. "It's hard to imagine that we're in the middle of a major city."

"It reminds me of the gardens at home. Sammy and I would disappear for hours playing some made up game. The only time we would hear someone was when Maria came searching to call us in for food."

"It does remind me of your garden. Especially the green expanse of lawn, the huge shady trees and the flower beds."

I had once daydreamed about lying on a picnic rug in that garden with light filtering through the trees. I would be reading a book with a dog lying beside me. The lush lawn beneath us like a plush carpet. Peace enveloped us. The only sound was the light breeze rustling the leaves and the dog's content breathing. I smiled at the thought.

We joined hands again as we made our way to The Calyx. As soon as we touched, my heart did the same jolt and my skin tingled. I tried to immerse myself in the serenity of the gardens rather than the racing of blood in my arteries, and the questions running through my mind; like, what the hell was I doing?

I breathed the freshness deep into my lungs and imagined it being released into every cell, all the way to my extremities. The peacefulness of it settled into my soul. Our soft footsteps on the path, the faint sound of mowers in the distance, birds calling from the trees, all relaxed me. And we walked in silence, encapsulated by it all.

The Calyx was an amazing structure, perfectly circular. Stark steel white posts surrounded the circumference, rising five metres into the air before bending in a ninety-degree angle, extending into the centre in a pattern of precision. A perfect geometric shape. The ideal place to hide a treasure. In the centre sat a grass island with palm trees stretching into the air above. A pond surrounded the round island's circumference, followed by rings of garden, white stone, dark grey stone, and light grey stone. All perfect circles, radiating out from the centre.

"Do you think if we looked at it from above that it would look like the iris of an eye?" I asked, as we stood next to the pond.

Shepherd stared at the steel structure above us. "I reckon it would. The island would be the pupil." He turned full circle. "If you stared at this long enough you would feel hypnotised."

"No time for staring, let's look for this treasure."

Shepherd and I walked around the pond in opposite directions, searching the garden and water for anything that looked out of place. My hand felt empty without his, as if our sudden detachment left me lost in the wilderness. We took our time, looking closely, examining every last detail.

Nothing. There was nothing.

Shepherd

"I THOUGHT for sure there would be something here," I said to Tara, frowning, when we met back together. She sighed; her disappointment as evident as mine.

"We have three more water features to go. Murphy's Law says it will be the last one we look at," she said, giving me an encouraging smile.

"Probably."

I took her hand again. The spark I felt spurred me on. Together we were a team, and together we would not be defeated. By the time we got to the last fountain, I was smiling to myself at the irony. It was Cupid Fountain—Cupid, the Roman God of Love. The reason I was here. That would be something Sammy would do. We circled around the pool once, twice, three times and could not find anything that could be classed as a treasure. Cupid watched the whole time, silent, considering.

I ran my hand through my hair and sighed.

"How could we have missed it?" I said to Tara. Her blond hair was in a ponytail today, and she twirled it absently. She walked around the fountain again, her eyes downcast as she concentrated.

"We've checked all the water features we were told about. I don't think we missed anything." She kept walking. "Should we check them all again?"

"I guess so. Maybe we need to look at everything, not just things that seem out of place."

By the time we had examined the water features in reverse order the afternoon was upon us. And we had still found no treasure.

"Maybe we need to find a worker to double check we've covered them all," Tara suggested.

"Let's do that."

We walked absentmindedly, not speaking, until we spotted a gardener kneeling in a flower bed surrounded by blue and white flowers.

"Excuse me," Tara said as we approached.

The middle-aged man with greying hair stood up and smiled. The thick, earthy scent of the mulch he had been spreading around the delicate flowers infused the air.

"Yes, how can I help you?" he asked as he wiped his hands on a rag.

"We're competing in a scavenger hunt, and we think our treasure is in a water feature. We've checked the ones marked on our map. Could you please tell us if we missed any?"

Tara handed the map to the gardener and he examined it.

"The feature needs to be a geometric shape," I added.

"The ones circled are the only ones that match that description."

Tara and I looked at each other.

"Maybe the element isn't water. Maybe it's earth," I said.

"Are there any display areas of dirt that are in a shape?" Tara asked. Her forehead wrinkled and I imagined she felt the same as me, how or why would dirt be displayed like that?

"No, nothing comes to mind."

Tara's shoulders slumped as she bit her lip.

"Maybe we chose the wrong place," I said to Tara.

"Maybe. But the clues all pointed to the Botanic Gardens."

The gardener looked between us.

"Perhaps you should try the Blue Mountains Botanic Gardens," he suggested.

Tara and I looked at each other. I went through the clues in my head one by one. "I don't think so. One of the clues said it was established in the 1800s. The garden opened in 1987."

"That is true of the Botanic Gardens, but its history dates back to the 1800s."

Tara and I glanced at each other and then looked at the gardener.

"I worked there for a number of years, so I know the history. A land grant was given out in 1830," he explained.

"Do you think the clue could be that broad?" Tara asked me.

"It didn't say established in its current form. It merely said established."

"Shepherd, we're lawyers. We should know that things are not always written literally and can be open to interpretation."

The gardener looked between us. Tara's eyes sought mine. I stepped close to her and took both her hands.

"It's OK, Tara." I turned to the gardener. "Can you tell me what time it closes please?"

"The visitor centre closes at 4:30."

"How long does it take to get there?"

"At least an hour and a half, depending on traffic."

I looked at my watch, by the time we got back to the hotel and out to the gardens it would be closed. "We'll have to go tomorrow."

"But we will have lost a day," she said.

"It's OK. We may have lost a day today, but we'll gain one

somewhere else. As of tomorrow, we still have sixteen days, we're doing good."

I pulled her towards me and kissed the top of her head. Taking her face between my hands, I looked at her and, without falter, said again, "It's OK."

As soon as she nodded acknowledgement, her shoulders relaxing, I leant in and kissed her. It was quick. Not even a second. But my lips were tingling from the contact. I felt more hope today than I had in five long years. I looked into her green eyes, totally mesmerised. Licking my lips, I bent my head towards hers as her face tilted up to mine. My lips were ready to take hers, to devour them.

The gardener cleared his throat. Distracted, I drew away from Tara, my heart thrummed in my chest. Colour rose in her cheeks as she watched me. I took the map he was holding towards us.

"Good luck."

"Thanks for your help."

Well, some of it anyway. I could have done without the interruption.

<hr>

Tara

"I WANT to show you something before we catch the ferry back," I said to Shepherd, detouring off our path to Circular Quay. As darkness was settling, we made our way to one of the city parks. People were huddled on chairs or against trees. People dressed in dirty clothes. Some of them wearing clothes so big they hung off their shoulders and hips. A few were holding signs asking for money.

"During the day a lot of the homeless sleep, tucked away in corners or even out in the open on the grass. It's safer then, in broad daylight. They're less likely to be robbed of their meagre possessions or assaulted."

Shepherd looked around at the mismatch of people. You could tell which ones were afflicted by drugs. Some walked around in a stupor, not being able to connect on a human level. Others walked around with frenzied eyes and talking to themselves, their movements jittery.

"These are the people I want to help. But I want to help them before they become homeless, dejected, feeling unworthy."

He nodded while we continued walking.

"My grandparents took in a lot of people when we were younger. They lived in the shearer's quarters on the farm. These people were down on their luck, their marriages had broken up or they'd lost their way."

"How did your grandparents know who needed help?"

"Usually the police contacted them, or the church. Sometimes people turned up because they heard it was a sanctuary." I laughed. "If they thought they were coming to a holiday home, they were sadly mistaken. If you wanted to stay on the farm, there was only one way to do that, and that was to work. My grandfather, like any farmer, had an endless list of jobs."

We all contributed. Even when Zac and I moved there we had jobs. We were young then, the jobs easy, but they didn't stay that way.

"How long did they stay for?"

"Some couldn't hack it so they'd only stay a few days. A

few of them stayed for years. They became family and still visit Nan and Pop to this day. But the only way you could stay at all was to pass the Benny test. My grandparents always looked after our safety first, and if Benny didn't like you, there was no way you were staying."

A homeless man with holey jeans rested against a wall with his brown, shaggy terrier by his side. His sign asked for money to help feed his dog. I wouldn't give him money. It was something my grandparents taught me. They said it could be used for alcohol or drugs, but I would be happy to buy him food. As we approached and I slowed, his dog sat up and rested against his master's side. He looked to him for reassurance.

"Hello," I said, stopping in front of the man.

He regarded me with his dull blue eyes. His scruffy hair and beard were greying.

"Hi," he replied, his voice gravelly.

"What's your dog's name?"

"Billy." The dog's ears twitched at recognition of his name.

"Is it OK if I pat him?"

His blue eyes regarded me before he nodded. He put a comforting hand on Billy's neck. I moved towards them and crouched down when I was within reach. Shepherd stayed where he was, watching us.

"Hi, Billy," I said. I reached my hand out to him. He stretched his nose out to smell my hand.

"It's OK, Billy," the man said, his voice low and calm.

At his master's words, the dog's apprehension disappeared. He moved closer, leaning against me, accepting pats.

"Does Billy need some food?" I asked.

The man gave me a single nod.

"Do you need some food?"

Again, a single nod.

"Do you want to come with us and we'll buy you some?"

The man looked between me and Shepherd, uncertain. Shepherd reached out his hand to shake the man's. That simple gesture made my heart open that little bit more. So much for my mantra. Who was I kidding? The mantra no longer existed.

The man looked at Shepherd's hand, his jaw working, before taking it.

"I'm Shepherd. This is Tara. If you don't want to lose your spot, we can get what you need."

I kept my attention on Billy. How did Shepherd know that's what might be holding him back?

"No, no, this spot isn't anything special."

"All right then, let's find a supermarket."

"There's one just up the road."

Shepherd

I WATCHED as Tara helped the man put his pillows, blankets, and sign into his trolley. Billy stayed by his master's side the whole time. Tara didn't flinch away from anything he handed to her, regardless of cleanliness.

"Shepherd and I are competing in a scavenger hunt," Tara said as we walked towards the supermarket.

"Really? What do you win?"

"Some money. We missed finding our treasure today. We got the location wrong."

"That's a shame. Where'd you think it was?"

I walked behind them, watching their body language. Both of them were open to each other, turning to the other when talking, making eye contact.

"The botanical gardens. But it appears we chose the wrong garden."

"Were you meant to go to the one at Mount Tomah?"

"Yeah. The clues were a bit tricky."

He nodded, and after a moment said, "I'm Greg, by the way."

"Nice to meet you, Greg," Tara said, giving him a big smile.

When we arrived at the supermarket, I assessed the situation. They wouldn't allow Billy inside, but I didn't want to leave him alone tied to a chair or leave Greg's trolley either. This was all he owned, and I didn't want it to be stolen.

"How about I sit here with Billy and you and Tara go in?"

Greg looked between us and Billy, his mouth in a tight line and eyes narrowed.

"Don't worry. I'm not going anywhere. You have my most precious thing. I won't leave without her."

He smiled then. It was a big toothy grin. He looked at Tara.

"Bit of a sweet talker, your man." Then he turned towards Billy and gave him a pat. "Billy, stay here."

Billy and I watched them walk away and didn't take our eyes off the doors, waiting for their return.

"So, Billy, how does one find a homeless man to look after?"

Billy cocked his head at me.

"Were you homeless as well?"

Billy didn't reply. He remained seated near the trolley, not taking his eyes off the doors. I didn't think there was any place Billy would rather be than with his master. They may not have had a roof over their head, but they had each other.

I moved closer to the trolley while talking to him. He turned, regarding me with his warm brown eyes. Without warning, he jumped onto the seat beside me, nudging my hand to say he wanted a pat. We sat there in silence, enjoying each other's company.

Billy stood up, his tail wagging, as Tara and Greg came out the doors. He turned his face towards mine and gave me a lick.

"Good boy, Billy," I said, patting his head.

"Have a Captain Cook at these two," Greg said, looking at me and giving Tara a nudge.

What the hell did Captain Cook have to do with anything?

"He's like a one-eyed cat watching two mouse holes."

OK. I think I understood that reference. He must mean I was busy searching for them.

Tara laughed. "The pair of them stand out like dog's balls."

What? Dog's balls? I didn't remember anything special about Billy's.

Now Greg was chuckling along with her.

"Australian speak again? You can't expect me to believe this is how you normally speak."

"Pig's arse it's not!" Greg said.

"Seriously? What's anything got to do with a pig's arse?"

They both glanced at each other and laughed.

"I don't know," Tara said. "It's just something we say when we don't agree with someone."

I shook my head, bewildered.

"You should give him a fair go. He seems ridgey-didge." Greg put his arm around Tara's shoulder and gave her a squeeze.

I don't know if I'd ever understand what they were saying.

"I reckon he's a keeper," Greg said to Tara. "Only someone with a good heart would get a kiss from Billy."

Tara smiled. "Yeah, I reckon he is."

My heart did a happy dance. Seventeen days, that's how long I had to convince her, not only to say I was a keeper but to actually keep me. Seventeen days left to raise the money. Seventeen days for her to open up to me and tell me why she left. I would not push her, unless absolutely necessary. I wanted this to come from her.

Billy looked between us and smiled while wagging his tail. Did he think I was a keeper too?

Tara took pity on me, and came over and took my hand. She gave me a kiss on the cheek. "Greg thinks I should give you a chance because you're the real deal."

"That's nice of Greg to say." I don't know how a stranger could have any influence on our relationship, but he did. And if he was saying good things about me, who was I to disagree?

Tara turned to Greg. "Why don't you get changed into your new clothes in the bathroom? Then we can take your old clothes to the laundromat to wash."

Bam! I just fell in love with her a little more.

SIXTEEN DAYS

Tara

NO MATTER WHAT I DID, I was finding it harder to stay away from the temptation that was Shepherd. When we hadn't found the treasure yesterday, and he told me it was OK, I believed him with every ounce of my being. I always believed him. He had never given me any reason not to. It was only me who had doubted. It wasn't even Shepherd I'd doubted. It was fate's cruel blow and its uncanny ability to visit me. I thought it would take him away, like Zac and my parents. Did I trust that cruel blow to stay away now?

"Are you ready?" Shepherd asked as he turned off the car.

The question was simple enough. But without him knowing it, it held a lot more than just a trip to the Blue Mountains Botanic Gardens. Was I ready to give my love for Shepherd a second chance? My heart beat fast and I was shaky as I delivered my answer.

"Yes."

As we stepped onto the back deck of the visitor's centre, I

sucked in my breath. The garden stretched out before us, beautifully in touch with the landscape. The rock gardens directly below us were interspersed with shrubs of grey-green hugging the ground, through to taller luscious proteas with dark, matte green leaves. No species dominated the scene. Garden beds featured rocks of all shapes and sizes with paths winding between them.

Beyond the rock garden was a spiral rock wall path, leading down to the next level of the garden, beyond which was a woodland of pines and conifers. A valley dipped beyond those woodlands and from the other side emerged the panoramic view of the Blue Mountains. Trees covered the mountains from base to top and stretched all the way to the horizon. The ruggedness contrasted against the pale blue sky.

The plants in the foreground, bright and airy, were not crowded but were given enough space to shine in their own right, to be appreciated for their uniqueness. Round, flat, tall, skinny, different shades of green, all disappeared into the solidarity of the bush, the trees indistinguishable. The only change of the trees on the mountains was where they were accentuated by the dips and rolls of the gullies. The mountains actually looked blue.

The noise of the cars along the road behind us was lost in the silence of the surroundings. Everything was still, not even a breeze rustled the leaves. The quietness embraced me, settling into every part of my being. Recentring me. Calming me.

Shepherd broke my trance when he said softly, as if we were in church, "Ready?"

I turned my eyes from the wonder before us to the man smiling at me and nodded. Armed with our map, I made my way down the stairs to the Foundation Terrace. Stretching the length of the terrace was a slate grey, rectangular pond, behind which stood a rock wall. The wall itself was pure mastery, fashioned like the dry rock walls of old. The face of the wall was almost flat. Each rock, ranging in colour from orange to almost black, fitted together perfectly like they were made to sit together for centuries.

"Imagine how long it must have taken to fit all these pieces together," I said.

"It would be like doing a puzzle with no picture to follow."

I glanced along the length of the pool. "Do you want to start searching up the other end and we'll meet in the middle?"

He nodded and made his way to the other end while I examined the wall.

"I think I see something," Shepherd called out over the sound of the waterfall.

I turned towards him as he stopped. Leaning his hands on the side of the pond he peered closer at the water. I joined him and stared at the base of the pond, my skin prickling in anticipation. There was something blue tucked against the edge, shimmering. Shepherd reached in and pulled it out. It was a glass ball, as big as a grapefruit, coloured green and blue. He turned it around in his hands. Floating around on the inside, submersed in liquid, were our initials.

I sighed, releasing tension as lightness filled my limbs. I looked up at Shepherd. I wanted him to kiss me. My lust was a coiled snake, lifting its head, stretching out towards him. I knew what his lips felt like. I knew what he tasted like. I'd remembered it for five years and now I yearned for it more than ever. Musk from his cologne was sexy as hell. My skin tingled as I breathed it in deeper, drawing it deep into my lungs.

I took a step toward him. As he reached out and curled his hand around the back of my neck, heat surged through my body. The snake lunged and didn't stop until our bodies rammed together. Shepherd's lips met mine, hard, punishing, like he was a drowning man fighting for his last breath and he would extricate it from me. Our bodies pressed into each other, mimicking the desire of our lips. Everywhere he touched my skin burned. The snake coiled and twisted; the lust trying to break free as want surged within me.

The crashing of our lips matched the harshness of our breath. His tongue plunged into my mouth. His unique sweetness mixed with the banana smoothie we had for breakfast danced across my tongue. He pressed his hardness against me and I moaned. I wanted him. Every part of my body wanted him. My hands made their way around his back and held him tight. The cotton of his t-shirt was soft under my insistent hands. The constant sound of the waterfall matched the rush of blood in my ears. Shepherd's breath grew ragged. I couldn't even remember what breathing was. I couldn't remember who I was.

He wrenched his lips away. His eyes opened slowly, glassy and soft.

"Fuck, I've missed you."

I couldn't reply. I didn't think I could formulate words. My only thought was I was home.

Shepherd

MY LIPS HAD FELT like they were possessed. Kissing Tara was exactly how I remembered it. It felt good. And now, I just wanted more. Everything. All of her.

I needed to tell her about the game. But I couldn't do that until I knew we had the money for her foundation secured. Sammy hadn't emailed back, and I didn't know if that was because he was hard at work or because he didn't have good news for me. Had he asked everyone on the list I gave him? Had they agreed to contribute? I needed the three million dollars if I was going to make it right.

I hated holding the truth back, but I didn't feel like I had much choice. The foundation was important to her. But not only that, it was a good cause. Reducing drug abuse would reduce crime. It would reduce the number of people wasting away in our jail system or on the streets, continuing the devastating cycle.

We sent a photo of our find as soon as we got to the car. As we made our way back to Sydney, we got a reply. Tara read it out to me.

You two look as happy as a kid in a candy store. Your next set of clues will arrive shortly.

I cringed at the familiarity of the comment. It was such a Sammy thing to say. But Tara said nothing. When I glanced at her, she was touching her upturned lips.

"That was one hell of a kiss," I said, and waited for her reaction.

She smiled wistfully. "Uh-huh."

That was promising. No sudden ground rule saying we

couldn't kiss. I grinned. This new rule breaker, Shepherd, could be onto a winner.

We drove in silence. Even though I was sitting right next to her, it was too far away. Reaching over, I rested my hand on her leg. It took all of my willpower to keep it still, instead of letting it trail up her leg, closer to... I moved in my seat, trying to adjust myself, as my hard-on pressed against my zip. I needed some relief. Soon.

A text came through with the next set of clues.

Hunt 3
We are the oldest in the world.
A windy road will bring you directly
    here.
We have crystal formations and clear
    underground rivers.
C is for ceiling and G is for ground.
We were a bushranger's hideout.

"A windy road. You're going to like that," I said, remembering our trip to the mountains during winter break while at grad school.

"I just need to watch where we're going and I should be fine."

"You can drive, if it makes you feel better."

She turned her face to mine. "You remember that? That drive to the mountains?"

"How could I forget? I've never seen anyone turn green like that."

She laughed and turned in her seat towards me.

"You were so worried, but you couldn't pull over."

"And I started to go slow, hoping it would help, and the line of cars behind us got impatient."

I shook my head. It was terrible to watch someone feel so ill and have no control, no way to help.

"And when you finally found a spot to pull over, I fell out of the car and lay in the snow."

"And all you could do was stare up at the sky."

"I was trying to reset my inner balance."

"Really? Is that what you call it?"

She gave me a light punch.

"And I was giving a running commentary on how your face was changing colour."

She blushed. "Green. Yellow. Pasty white. Something resembling a human."

"Resembling human." I chuckled, remembering the look on her face like I'd just insulted her.

"Then you let me drive and all was good with the world again. Or at least my equilibrium."

She took hold of my hand and smiled at me. And just as she had that day, lying on the side of the road, she took my breath away.

Rule number one – demolished.

When we arrived back at the apartment we sat down to dinner and reviewed the clues, typing them into the laptop.

"Uh. These results tell us the oldest things in Sydney but don't say they are the oldest in the world," Tara said, before taking a bite of her burger.

"Maybe Wikipedia will have something," I said as I clicked on the link.

She leant closer to read the screen. Her warmth embraced me.

"Nope. Oldest library in Australia, oldest parkland. Wait, this says that Sydney Airport is one of the oldest continually operating airports in the world."

"But not the oldest. Maybe we should write it down, anyway. We don't want to get caught out again," I said.

"The Royal National Park is the second oldest national park in the world," she said, adding it to the list.

"That's impressive for a country so young. I mean, it's not young, Aboriginals were here for 50,000 years. But young as in settled."

"Two hundred and thirty years of settlement. And most of those not so happy for our indigenous Australians."

I nodded. There was nothing else to say. I'd read the stories. "I'll search for a couple more pages and see if anything else shows up."

I scrolled and scrolled.

"Nothing?" she asked.

"Nothing."

"OK. Next clue - windy road." She stretched in her seat, arching her back, accentuating her breasts. I turned away and concentrated on the screen.

"Look, it mentions Bells Line of Road. That's where the Blue Mountains Botanic Gardens were," I said.

"I still can't get over that name—Bells Line of Road. It's so bizarre," she said, laughing.

"I wonder why it's called that," I said, ready to investigate further.

She shook her head at me. "Now is not the time to get distracted."

She gave me a smile and looked at the screen. She was right, once we started looking at why the road was called that we would probably veer off onto other weird road names. We could be here all night looking up random stuff. I looked back at the screen and returned to the task at hand. "Jenolan Caves Road is another one to add to the list."

"None of the clues match up so far. Let me take over so you can finish eating," she said. She moved her plate out of the way and slid the laptop across.

She typed in the next clue—crystal formations and underground rivers. "Just about every link points to the Jenolan Caves."

Her eyes were wide and sparkling when they turned towards me. I hoped this was it. It would be good not to repeat what happened yesterday. Then I shook my head. Sometimes I forgot that this wasn't even a real game. She typed away.

"Ok, the caves are the oldest in the world, 340 million years old. They have crystal formations and clear underground rivers. The road is windy. And it was known to be a bushranger's hideout."

"What about that other clue? C is for ceiling; G is for ground?"

"I'll google it."

I held my breath while she typed, hoping the answer we wanted would be revealed. And it was, straight away - stalactite has a C for ceiling, and stalagmite has a G for ground.

"Stalactites and stalagmites."

"Caves."

"It makes perfect sense," she said, her grin wide as she leant over to hug me. Her softness was wrapped in my arms and her breasts pushed against my chest. I wanted to pull her into my lap, so she was straddling me, to feel her against me. So close, she would be so close. I wanted her, all of her. My breath hitched.

Tara

WHEN I RELEASED SHEPHERD, he reached out to tuck some loose strands of hair behind my ear. His intimate touch sent a shiver across my skin. Was I ready for this? To risk my heart? I didn't think I could deny it—him—for much longer.

I didn't want to deny him. The only reason I left in the first place was because of what I saw. Because I was afraid he would die. But he wasn't on drugs now. And the more time I spent with him, the more I remembered why I loved him. He had depth. Passion. And my heart.

"It's Sunday night. Do you want me to do the dishes while you ring home?" he asked.

After all these years he still remembered the ritual.

"Thank you. I wasn't sure if I would be able to call them."

I took my phone out to the balcony and dialled the number. I put the phone on loudspeaker knowing Nan and Pop would have theirs on loudspeaker too. It was easier to hear them that way. The thought Shepherd may be able to hear us disappeared when they answered the phone.

"Hello," Nan said, her voice surprised.

"Hi, Nan."

"Tara, sweetie, I wasn't sure you'd be able to call us."

"We are allowed to use our phones, just not to get help

with the scavenger hunt. We had to download an app that records our conversations to make sure we aren't cheating."

"Where are you?" Pop asked in his deep voice.

"I didn't go far. We're in Sydney."

"That's a surprise," Nan said. "I thought it would be some strange, exotic place."

"So did I."

"How has it been going?" Pop asked.

"Good. There's really no advantage to being Australian. The clues aren't any easier. Our first hunt went well. Our second one, we went to the wrong place, but we got it the next day."

"Did they explain the requirement to win?" Pop asked. He was so astute.

"Yes, we have five hunts to complete in twenty days. The first one to complete them wins. But we have no idea who the other teams are or how they're going."

"Hmm." I pictured him sitting next to Nan, rubbing his chin.

"Regardless of if you win or lose, we are proud of you, Tara. You're doing this for a good cause. Your parents would be proud, too."

I imagined they would be, but as the years passed, I felt less connected to them. I missed them. I remembered how happy we were as a family. But it was so long ago. They were alive for a quarter of my life. Would I feel the same about Zac one day? I hated to think of the possibility. I couldn't believe the memories I held so close could grow faint. The ones I had of Shepherd hadn't, and I'd only known him for twelve months.

"Nan's right, they would be proud. Not just about this

competition, but everything you've done."

"Because of you," I said.

Nan changed the subject. "How much will you win?"

"Three million. Imagine how many people I can help with that!" I got tingles every time I thought about it.

"You could keep the foundation running for years. What's your team like?"

"I just have one partner."

"Is she nice?"

"'She' is a he."

I wasn't entirely sure why I was being so vague. There was no point.

"Is he nice?"

"Yes, Shepherd is nice."

I glanced toward the kitchen. Shepherd was watching me closely. I could take the phone off loud speaker, but what was the point? I couldn't keep hiding things from him. I'd done that before and it hadn't turned out well.

"Shepherd?" Nan asked.

"As in Shepherd Bell III?" Pop may have aged, but he was still as sharp as a tack.

"Yes."

There was a pause. I knew exactly what they were doing at that moment. They were looking at each other and having a silent conversation. Just as they had the day my parents died and many times thereafter.

Pop spoke, "Tara, you listen to me."

When didn't I? But I knew when he started with those words, he was going to say something I didn't want to miss. Just like the day I told him I was going to the States for grad school. *'Tara, you listen to me. Go out there and live. Don't let life's tragedies hold you back.'* I did what he said, sort of. I just forgot that living meant sharing your inner self.

His voice brought me back to the present. "The good God has put that man back in front of you for a reason."

I looked up at Shepherd who was looking straight back at me. My heartbeat increased. He'd heard every word and was listening still.

"Yes, Pop."

"Not many people get a second chance at love. You of all people know life is too short to waste it."

I did. I'd wasted five years already. I couldn't waste any more.

"Yes, Pop."

I was still looking at Shepherd. Our eyes locked, the colour rising in my cheeks.

"Loss can make you weary but it shouldn't stop love."

"What Pop is trying to say, Tara, love, is that it has been five years and you're still in love with that man."

Shepherd and I stared at each other, neither of us moving an inch. My insides were somersaulting. She said what I'd been too afraid to admit for years.

"You need to make things right."

I gulped. And tore my eyes away from Shepherd. "Yes, Nan."

I needed to make things right. I needed to. Me.

"I love you girl. We look forward to speaking to you next week."

"Bye, Pop. Bye, Nan."

They were gone.

Me. It was up to me.

I knew it was. I was the one who'd left without a word. I was the one who'd left him.

I sat and looked at the sky as the last rays of light disappeared.

Shepherd

SHE LOVES ME? She has loved me all this time? My skin prickled as adrenaline soared through my body. I placed my hands on the bench to steady myself.

All this time I'd wondered what I'd done wrong. I felt unworthy of love.

And now I found out that she did love me.

Tara stayed on the balcony, barely moving. I couldn't leave this all up to her. She needed my help. Wiping my hands on the tea towel, I tossed it onto the bench and walked outside. Sitting on the chair next to her, I reached over and gave her hand a squeeze.

She didn't say anything. She stared out at the dark sky dotted with faint stars; stars never shone as brightly in the city. Her breaths were uneven and I could feel tremors through her hands.

How could I help her? I didn't want to push her. I could wait until she was ready. A lump formed in my throat at seeing her slumped shoulders. Should I ask her about loving me? I could make light of it. Say something about her offhanded quote at the supermarket being true. Maybe it would draw out the reason she left.

Or should I ask about her parents?

My mother died when I was young. Too young to remember her. When I told people, it didn't have a huge effect on me. It held no emotion. I guess her death shaped my life, but I never knew life with a mother. And I had Maria. She may have been a housekeeper, but both her and my dad had brought me up.

But I knew life with Tara and when she had left me, I had felt lost. I was alone even though there were people around me. If I felt like that as an adult, it would be a million times worse for a child who lost their parents.

"You never told me your parents died."

She took a deep breath. I expected her to move away, to take her hand from mine. She had been running from telling me all of this time, I wasn't sure if she would stop now.

***

Tara

SHEPHERD'S VOICE held no accusation.

I glanced at him. He was watching me closely.

I took a deep breath. It was over twenty years ago, but sometimes it felt like yesterday. Shepherd shifted in his seat. What did he think of me for not telling him any of this before? What would I have thought of him if he had kept something like this from me? I would have been hurt and confused, for starters. I didn't want Shepherd to feel that way.

"No, I haven't really told anyone. I can still remember it clear as day. My grandparents were looking after us; they let us stay up to wait for our parents. We heard a car pull up in the driveway and footsteps come to the door. A knock sounded. I didn't think at the time that it was weird for my parents to knock.

"We were so excited we ran to the door. Benny was right behind us, wagging his tail and jumping around. Two police officers were standing where I expected to see my mum and dad. My grandparents were right behind us. My nan's sharp intake of breath was harsh. I can remember how her voice sounded funny when she told us to wait in the lounge room. It's weird the things you remember about the day that changed your life."

My hand was sweating in Shepherd's. I wanted to withdraw it, to wipe the sweat away. But his hand grounded me. It tied me to now. To him. I was afraid if I took it away, I'd get lost in the memory, and I wouldn't be able to finish what I'd started.

"Zac and I didn't understand what was going on. It felt exciting for us to see real live policemen at our door. We hid around the corner and listened."

I remembered how Benny had stood right beside me and I had rested my hand on his head. He must have sensed something was wrong before the police even spoke. He had pushed himself against my leg and rubbed his head into my hand. The police had given some introductions and confirmed my grandparent's identity.

"Then the big policeman said, 'There's been an accident. I'm sorry to tell you that Matt and Elanor have been killed.' Those words didn't compute in my mind. Nan howled like someone had torn her heart out. She was the quietest, most reserved person I have ever known. The sound drew Zac and I out of the shadows. Benny came with us. He stood between us and Zac and I held hands over his back.

"We stood there and watched as Pop broke down. A grown man, as strong as nails, brave and resilient, cried from a broken heart. Benny whimpered. I will never forget that scene until the day I die."

Tears rolled down my cheeks. I thought I had cried all the tears I could over their deaths. It had been years since they died. Sure, tears sprung into my eyes sometimes, but they no longer fell. It surprised me the trauma was still so raw.

"I don't know if we understood what was happening, but Zac and I stood there, clutching each other. The police officers alerted my grandparents to our presence. Pop took Nan's face in his hands. They communicated between themselves without saying a word, then turned to us and took us into their fold."

Tears continued to flow. The way Pop held Nan's face that day reminded me of how Shepherd had held mine in the gardens when we had gotten the clues wrong. Just that simple touch had reassured me. And now, when he reached over and cupped the back of my head, it had the same effect. I calmed my breathing and waited for my tears to disappear before I looked at him.

Shepherd

I LISTENED TO TARA INTENTLY.

A lump settled into the pit of my stomach. Her eyes were distant, she stared beyond the balcony as she spoke. I gazed down at her hands, not wanting to distract her from her story. Or myself, for that matter. My eyes rose to her face when she finished and she tore her gaze from the sky to face me and give me a small smile.

I didn't let her hand go.

"I—" What was there that I could possibly say?

I caressed her face, hoping it conveyed everything I wanted to say. Leaning her cheek into my hand, she sighed.

Saying I'm sorry didn't feel adequate. Did I need to say something? I should. More than anything I wanted to lift her into my lap and hold her. Before I had the chance, Tara stood up, leaned down to give me a kiss and said, "Goodnight."

Her arms hung limply at her side as she walked to her room. I got up to follow. Did she want me to be with her? Maybe she needed some time alone. Standing in the middle of the dining room, I watched her go, and when she didn't turn to look at me, I knew the answer. I went to my room.

I lay there hours later thinking through it all. We had been together for twelve months. I fell for her the day she stepped foot into our Immigrants' Rights classroom. I had known none of what she'd told me. I knew of her grandparents and how they helped people. I knew she'd had a happy childhood. I knew she had a brother she loved. But this loss she had experienced, I didn't have the slightest knowledge of that. Why? If she loved me, why wouldn't she share it with me?

If she had told me of her loss before, could I have helped her? I thought so. I could have helped her heal. But I was never given that chance.

My bedroom door opened and Tara entered the room. Without making a sound, she made her way to my bed and hopped in beside me. The person who I considered the strongest in the world lay beside me, fragile and forlorn.

I rolled over and put my arm around her, savouring the

smell of her vanilla shampoo. As she relaxed into me, I kissed the back of her head and held her close.

This wasn't just about winning her back anymore. This was about me showing her I was worthy of her love. How could I be worthy if I didn't tell her the truth? But I couldn't until I knew I could make her dream come true. It felt like the truth hinged on three million dollars.

FIFTEEN DAYS

Tara

AS SHEPHERD SAT NEXT to me for our three-hour drive to Jenolan Caves, I thought about our past relationship. Not telling Shepherd about Zac was a betrayal. By never allowing him to share my hurt and pain, I was keeping a part of myself from him. And by doing that, I was stopping us from having that ultimate bond.

I had told him about my parents. Now was the time to tell him about Zac. To tell him everything.

"Shepherd."

"Yeah?"

"I want to tell you about Zac." I inhaled shakily.

There. It was out. No going back on it now. I had no idea how this would go. I'd never told anyone the complete story. About my failure. Not even my grandparents. I didn't want them to feel the immense guilt and pain I felt. Because they would. Even though it was all out of their control, they still felt some responsibility. I needed to protect them. They'd suffered enough.

"I don't know where to start, really."

I paused. The car whizzed past the trees on the side of the road. I needed to tell him everything in one big hit. It would be a long story but we had three hours. Shepherd waited patiently for me to start. He reached over and gave my leg a squeeze. A small gesture that fortified my resolve.

"You know we were close. I've told you about the games we played. We were that close from the day I was born; he was just over a year old then. My parents told me he doted on me from the day I came home. Whenever I was awake, he would talk to me and play with me. I'm not sure how much playing a baby could do or a one-year-old for that matter, but apparently, we interacted a lot. Obviously, I had no idea what he was saying, but I hung onto every word. As soon as I could walk, he took me on adventures."

I smiled. A lot of the memories from when we were children had faded but I could still remember Zac holding my chubby little hand and how small it looked in his. And the way I looked up at his adoring face. The way he would smile back down at me. That smile said, 'I've got you. I've always got you'.

"We graduated to scavenger hunts when I was around three, inventing clues and hunting for treasure. At that age, he came up with the clues, but I soon learnt. Maybe it was those games that set us up for a profession as lawyers. We didn't just want to try cases—we wanted to investigate, like forensic lawyers."

I glanced at the sky thinking of those scavenger hunts. When Benny was alive, he would have the best time following us around. We'd incorporate things for him to do too, like follow scents or dig holes to find the next clue. We played them all the way through university as well, getting our friends to make teams and join in the fun.

"Our parents died when I was seven. Zac and I were practically inseparable after that. For a long while we slept in the same bed together with Benny between us making sure we were safe. Zac finished high school a year before me but waited, working on the farm, so we could go to uni together. We were all we had left. And together we would stay."

Pausing, I listened to the next set of directions from my phone. Shepherd said, "That makes sense."

"In 2011, he heard about Bitcoin. He thought it would be the next big thing. He was into that sort of thing, new technology, digital cash and how it would change the world. He invested $10,000 of our trust money from my parent's life insurance. He knew what he was talking about. When uni finished, our $10,000 investment was worth four million dollars.

"The money went to his head. We'd never been rich. We never wanted for anything, but we didn't live a life of luxury either."

That four million dollars ruined my life and then became my saviour. It took Zac, but then gave me a reason to live by giving me the ability to help others. I knew I needed to tell the rest of the story. But it was becoming increasingly difficult to put my thoughts into words. I needed to make sure I said everything, but each sentence brought me closer to the inevitable end. The crushing end. I stared at the road, at the white centre line rushing past, as I tried to get my thoughts aligned.

Taking a deep breath, I continued. "But the problem wasn't that the money went to his head. If he had started spending money on *things,* it wouldn't have been so bad. It wouldn't have mattered. Suddenly he was popular and started partying. The next thing I knew, he was taking drugs."

My hands tightened on the steering wheel. I'd asked myself a thousand times or more how things had gone so wrong. How I could have stopped it all? At what point I should have pinpointed the problem? Stopped it before it had gotten out of hand? Asked my grandparents for help?

"Shepherd, I just don't understand it. We never took drugs. Never. Sure, our friends experimented, but we never gave it a second thought. We'd seen what it did to some people who came to live on the farm. We saw how it ruined their lives and stole everything from them, even their family. We drank sometimes. What teenager doesn't? But he was never addicted to alcohol. We could go for months without having a drink. So why, how, did he become addicted to drugs?"

I was clutching the steering wheel so tight, rigidness riddled my body so much that I was leaning forward in the seat, almost as if I were an old lady trying to see over the bonnet. Shepherd squeezed my leg again. I turned my head to look at him. Simply knowing he was there with me, for me, helped me sit back in the seat, willing the tenseness to leave.

"That's the problem with drugs though, isn't it? Sometimes all it takes is one hit. And that's what it was like for Zac. He started with just one and it snowballed until he was taking it all the time just to get high. From party drugs to meth in a few short weeks."

All the time. It was all the time.

"I tried to reason with him. We both knew how bad drugs

were. We'd spoken about it openly. But he wouldn't listen. I'd stay awake constantly, trying to wait until he came off his high, waiting to talk sense into him. Make him see reason. But the low was so bad. He was angry. His sleep patterns were off the wall and then came the depression. He couldn't pay attention. So, when he was high, he *wouldn't* listen, and when he was coming down, he *couldn't* listen."

My breath was ragged. I forced my words out.

"I didn't tell my grandparents. I should have, but I didn't want them to worry. They could have helped. I still haven't told them all of it."

The memories were flooding back – Zac's pallid face, his wasted body, his gibberish. I'd kept them at bay for such a long time. Now it was like a fissure in a dam wall, and once the strength and integrity were compromised, there was no stopping the uncontrolled flow of emotions.

I found a safe place to pull over and got out of the car. My chest was going to explode. I wanted to scream, cry, hug myself, fall to the ground, punch someone. The tears streamed down my face and my throat constricted. I wanted to scream at God and ask him why. Demand a reason for taking my brother from me.

I saw Zac's face. His bloodshot, unseeing eyes. I cringed at the smell of someone barely human, the sweet and sour mixed in with a weird body odour. His lips were so dry from licking them, they were cracked. His skin scabbed in places from where he'd scratched himself raw. The sound of his voice, slurred beyond understanding or as high as a bird singing on a sunny day. I remembered it all. I was sure if I looked down, I would see him dead at my feet.

I couldn't help him. I couldn't. I tried.

Shepherd was beside me, encircling me in his arms as I sobbed, nearly to the point of vomiting. Zac was all I had left. He was gone. And I couldn't help him.

Shepherd held me tight, stopping me from falling to the ground.

"I couldn't help him, Shepherd. I tried, but he died right there in front of me."

I gulped the air in. My throat clogged.

"In that last moment, before the life left his eyes, he saw me. He saw *me*. And the love in his eyes was like it always was."

Shepherd

I SANK down to the ground with Tara in my arms and held her until she stopped crying. There was nothing I could do for her except comfort her in that moment. She had held all of this pain in for so long. Her façade was so controlled, now it was like an avalanche consuming her.

Her brother died right there in front of her. I couldn't even begin to imagine her anguish when the light left his eyes. Or the panic while she tried to revive him. Bile rose in my throat as I imagined her standing there, her green eyes vacant and red from crying, her face twisted in pain, when the paramedics declared him dead.

How many nights after that didn't she sleep? Did she see his face whenever she closed her eyes? Or did she sleep and hope to never wake?

She stayed in my arms, her blond hair falling wildly

around her shoulders. I held her tight, rubbing her back, keeping her in the moment with me. Her breathing was still ragged as she clutched the front of my shirt.

I wanted to tell her it wasn't her fault. But how do you convince someone of that? Her pain was so real, so raw, even after all this time. Was it because she never spoke about it? And because she never spoke about it, she never received absolution? It was time for her to start healing and I would do everything in my power to help her.

I wanted to show her how my love could strengthen her, just like her love strengthened me.

Tara

SHEPHERD and I stood next to Jenolan Caves House, the four storeys towering above us. It reminded me of an alpine retreat. A red, terracotta tiled roof held many decorative gables. The façade below was cream and there were multi-paned windows everywhere. Porticos extended from verandas, inviting people to enter heavy double wooden doors. Set within a valley, with trees climbing the hills surrounding us. We were in a fairy-tale world away from modern Sydney.

Shepherd and I walked into our hotel room. He'd asked for a twin room, but there was no point—I would end up sleeping in his bed anyway.

The cave tour we were going on had been cancelled due to a malfunction with the lighting, so we'd rebooked for the following day. We were unprepared for an overnight stay and didn't even have a change of clothes.

I sat on the king bed and looked around. The room was elegantly appointed with furniture akin to the federation era. Heavy green curtains hung in the bay windows. In front of the windows was a small sitting area with two chairs and a table. Deep red wainscoting and cream walls gave the feeling of old-world charm. It was simple but stylish.

My stomach tightened as Shepherd sat behind me. I had told him things over the past two days that I hadn't shared with anyone. But it still wasn't enough. I needed to tell him why I'd left.

I guess I didn't really have to. He seemed to have forgiven me. But, how could he? That was just being naive. He deserved to know, and I was not giving us the best chance of a future by hiding it. That's if he *wanted* a future with me. For Pete's sake, I had just relived the worst moment of my life, why was this so hard?

I sat further back on the bed, leaning on the headboard and drawing my knees up to my chest. Shepherd silently moved into position beside me. We both stared at the wall in front of us. Was his heart beating as fast as mine?

Regardless of if he wanted a future with me or not, holding back this last piece wasn't fair. I didn't know how to start.

As usual, Shepherd did. "Why did you leave, Tara?"

I broke out into a sweat. "I was scared."

"Of what?"

"Of losing you."

"So, you left me instead?"

A hundred thoughts and images floated through my head. Shepherd being so high he hadn't even noticed when I entered the room. Zac's face staring up at me, replaced by

Shepherd's. The way I ran from that house as if being chased by my worst nightmare. I couldn't even remember if I'd cried.

I was crying now.

"I saw you, Shepherd. At the house, on the day of graduation. You were as high as a kite. I couldn't do it. I couldn't stay and watch you die." It sounded so irrational. Just because I saw him take drugs once, it didn't mean it was going to kill him. But the loss of Zac was too raw for logic.

"I'm sorry, Tara."

What was he apologising to me for? I was the one who ran. I was the one who left him without saying a word. I wrung my hands together. "What?"

"I'm sorry you didn't trust me enough."

My stomach bottomed out. I stood up and went to the window. Staring out at the trees, I clenched my teeth. What could I say? I couldn't deny it. He was right. I hadn't trusted him. I only gave him part of me.

"If you had trusted me, you would have told me about your parents and Zac. If you did, I wouldn't have broken some sacred promise I didn't know existed."

I turned to him.

"You never even gave me a chance."

He was right. We were set for failure because the foundation I had laid was practically non-existent.

"I know." My voice was shaky.

I'd treated him terribly. Like he was some sort of commodity. Playing with his feelings and heart as if there was no return on investment. Because there never would have been. He gave me his all and what I gave failed in comparison.

The tears were streaming now. Pop said I needed to make

this right. But, how could I? How could I expect Shepherd to forgive me?

He watched me as I stood there. I eyed the door, but I couldn't run. If I did, I'd run for the rest of my life. I couldn't keep running, especially from the person I loved. My stomach twisted. When I looked back at him, he shook his head, as if telling me not to do it.

"I'm scared, Shepherd."

He came to me and lifted my chin.

"I love you, Tara. I'm not going anywhere."

"That's not in your control."

Shepherd

TARA SHRUGGED out of my hold. As she tried to move away, I took hold of her shoulders and held her in place.

"Tara, I'm here now. And I intend to stay with you. That's all that's in my power to promise."

She pounded her fists against my chest before clutching my shirt. Her head thumped against my shoulder. My arms surrounded her as sobs racked her body. Her arms circled my back and held me tight.

It took minutes for her body to soften against mine. Her hands eventually made their way up my back and held onto my shoulders, leaving heat in their wake. Turning her face to mine, her soft lips kissed my jawline until they reached my mouth. Our kiss was slow, mouths moving in unison, tongues dancing the rumba. Desire burned in me.

She pressed against me, against my hardness. Reaching

under her shirt, I undid the clasp of her bra. Without hesitation, she lifted her shirt off, and her bra fell to the floor. Our lips were apart for a mere second before meeting again, open and eager.

I craved her skin against mine. I tore my shirt off. Looking down at her, I was completely distracted by her body, breasts and nipples. My hands were drawn to them and, as soon as my thumbs met her nipples, she moaned. I throbbed in my jeans. I'd imagined this moment so many times, but this was better than anything I'd pictured.

Her hands found my chest and made their way to the waistband of my jeans. She undid my button and zip and slid my jeans from my hips. I stepped out of them and my underwear soon followed.

Without missing a beat, she pulled hers off. I couldn't take any more of this slow stuff. There would be time to revel in her, moment by moment, inch by inch, later. I pushed her to the bed. As she lay before me, I took in every inch of her. Her breasts were fuller than I remembered, her curves rounder. The small beauty spot on the side of her breast matched my memory.

"Do you have protection?" she asked.

I nodded, grabbing my wallet off the table.

"I'm on the pill, but it's better to be safe."

I rolled the condom on. "I haven't had unprotected sex with anyone but you."

"Same."

Tara pushed herself further onto the bed, giving me a chance to stare a moment longer before lying beside her. I lifted myself on my elbow. Kissing along the base of her neck, I made my way across her collar bone to her breasts. Her body responded exactly the way I wanted: her back arched and the breath hitched in her throat. I couldn't wait any longer. Laying on top of her, I entered her, kissing her. She stiffened underneath me and gasped into my mouth. She was wet, but so tight. I braced my body, trying to gain some control.

"Are you OK?"

She nodded. Her soft hands held me tight. I moved slowly until she moved with me, her slickness around me. I needed to slow down. I lowered my head to hers so I could kiss that special spot under her ear, burying my face in her soft hair that had fanned out around her, taking in vanilla and clean linen. My lips found hers and I kissed her tenderly. When she opened her legs wide, I went in deeper. Her warm skin caressed me. The feel of her around me, her moans, her tightening sent me to the edge. I couldn't hold back. My whole body shook as I released inside her. I relaxed on top of her.

With her soft breath against my ear, she said, "I love you, Shepherd."

There was no one on this earth I loved, or would ever love, as much as Tara Hill.

FOURTEEN DAYS

Tara

KISSING SHEPHERD WAS nothing compared to having sex with him. Sex was divine. How had I lived without him? Without his body, his lips, the way he made me feel? He'd always made me feel safe, loved, the centre of his universe.

We hadn't even made it down to dinner, too busy enjoying each other for anything else. We fell asleep entangled, and we awoke the same way. I didn't want to leave his arms or the bed or the room, but checkout time was looming and we had a hunt to complete.

I tore myself away from him knowing a slow escape would be physically impossible. As I lay there beside him, willing myself to get up, wondering if I could actually walk, his hand took mine. We needed to get out of bed or else we never would. As I sat up, I felt the ache in my thighs. We'd had more sex last night than I'd had in years.

I could feel Shepherd's eyes on me as I made my way to the bathroom. Before I even made it into the shower, he was behind me, his lips caressing my neck. Goose bumps erupted over my skin as my core begged for him. I stepped in and he followed. The water awakened my body and my need for him. I took his nipple in my mouth, relishing the feel of it and the water passing over my lips, wetting them, causing them to slip over his skin. My hand moved down his smooth chest, found his hardness, and wrapped around it, as my lips found his neck. His moan made me want him even more. I ached for him. I loved this man with every part of my being.

Shepherd's hand reached between my legs, rubbing before his fingers slipped in. He pushed me against the wall, the cold tiles behind my back cooling the heat inside me for a mere moment. He pushed his leg between mine to get greater access. His dick went harder. My hand let go as he stepped between my legs and lifted me, pushing himself inside my core. I winced. All of the sex the night before had left me raw. He was so big, and each thrust was a mixture of pure pleasure and heated friction. His head was beside mine, his harsh breath coming quicker.

The freshness of the water was invigorating. If every sensory cell wasn't already wakened, Shepherd's wet body against mine sent them into overload. My heat enveloped his dick as he pushed in further. Everywhere he touched, desire burned. His ragged breathing in my ear sent me to another level. I wanted him now, today, forever. Shepherd made me brave in ways I didn't know were possible. I believed in life, love, him. Five years I'd wasted trying to repent by helping others without ever helping myself. I knew I had to do that now. And Shepherd could help make that happen by standing by my side. Maybe I wasn't ready five years ago, but I was ready now. For him, for a future.

His movement quickened and he held me closer, his thrusts going deeper. I held onto his strong shoulders, broader than they were five years ago. Everything about him was bigger, better, hungrier. I pulsated around him. My head banged onto the tile behind me as my core clenched and I called out his name. My body arched as tremors passed through it. Grunting, he grabbed my hips and thrust himself deep inside me, holding me there until he was empty.

Unwrapping my legs, I lowered my feet, not sure if I could hold my own weight. Shepherd was no help. I could feel his legs shaking against mine as he slumped against me. I held onto his shoulders while my legs steadied.

AS WE MADE our way through the cave, Shepherd kept glancing back at me. My stomach did little excited flips. Each time his eyes found mine, his shoulders relaxed. It was as if he thought I was some kind of apparition that would suddenly disappear, but I wasn't going anywhere. Fate had brought us back together again; it would take an army to tear us apart.

I admired the shawl formations beside the path, expertly lit to show the intricate layer of colours – oranges, yellows and reds glowing like a sunset. But my eyes were always drawn back to him.

The stalagmites and stalactites reminded me of melted wax, only thousands of years old. Some stalagmites stood taller than us, but still did not reach the ceiling. On the end of a stalactite, a drop of water hung precariously. But no matter how long I looked at it, it did not fall. Things here were in slow motion. When not distracted by the beauty around us, or Shepherd, I looked for what could be our treasure. I knew it couldn't be hidden past the path because we were not allowed to go beyond that point. The risk of damaging the caves was too great.

We crossed a bridge with an underground river beneath us. It was still and clear. More than any water I'd ever seen. Peering along the cave walls, I tried to get some clarity of where the water reached. Blue lights lit the water from below. It was disorienting. The reflection on the surface was a perfect replica of the cave roof.

Shepherd stood beside me, his hand covering mine on the railing. Warmth spread from his touch. He bent his head to kiss my lips softly, sending lightness through my body.

"We should check the railings along the bridge and walkway for the treasure," he suggested.

"What treasure?" a young boy with short brown hair and freckles asked.

"We're on a scavenger hunt and we're looking for the hidden treasure."

"Like pirates' treasure?" The boy's eyes widened.

Shepherd smiled at him. "No, not pirates' treasure."

"What sort of treasure then?"

"We don't know until we find it."

"Can I help?"

"Sure, but you can't touch anything beyond the path."

"OK."

He set off ahead of us checking every railing. He was stopped by the guide who asked what he was doing, and the boy pulled him down so he could whisper in the guide's ear. Nodding, the guide whispered back and pointed to the other end of the path. The boy's pace was as quick as it could be without breaking into a run.

I loved how Shepherd let the excited boy join us. He could have been selfish and kept the find for us, but that wasn't Shepherd. Shepherd didn't do selfish.

The boy searched until he arrived at a box which held the switches for the lights. His face lit up when he found something. He returned with a huge smile on his face as he handed us two padlocks joined together. I took them from him and saw that one lock had my initials and the other Shepherd's. What a strange treasure.

"Thanks, champ," Shepherd said, giving the boy's hand a shake. He walked off full of pride with his chin raised and his chest puffed out. When he reached the guide, he got a high five. The guide gave us a wink.

Shepherd

TARA'S steady breathing beside me told me she was sleeping soundly. I grabbed my phone off the bedside table and headed for the door. When I reached it, I looked back at her. She hadn't moved. I closed the door quietly behind me.

I checked my emails first. There was nothing from Sammy. My heart dropped. Did that mean he was having no luck raising the funds?

I dialled his number. He answered after two rings. "Shepherd, how are you?"

"Good. Really good."

"I'm glad that guy I found on the internet to plant the treasures has worked out."

"Yeah, he hasn't let you down. Three down, two to go."

"So, operation 'win back Tara' is going to plan?"

"It's better than I planned. I need to tell her about the game. I feel guilty."

"The fundraising is progressing," he said, slowly.

His evading comment made me suspicious, as did his lack of questions about what was happening with Tara and I.

"How much have we raised?"

"One point two million, with our money and Tara's entry fee."

Crap. That wasn't nearly enough. Sammy would be working hard on it. I didn't want him to feel bad for not reaching our goal or even half of our goal. "That's not bad for a few days' work."

"We have a bit of a problem." He let the statement hang in the air. My heartbeat quickened.

"What sort of problem?"

"Your dad knows what you're up to. He's not impressed."

I tried to keep my voice low so I didn't disturb Tara. "What exactly is he not impressed about?"

"I think he feels that you're tricking Tara and that it's not how a relationship should start."

"I know. It seemed like a good idea at the time." I stared out the window as a long sigh escaped my lips.

"You need to tell her, Shep."

I knew that. It had gone too far, but I didn't think I could stop this derailing train. "I know. I want to raise more money first. This is important to her."

"Don't you think the longer you keep the secret the worse it will be?"

I ran a hand through my hair. How did I ever think this would be a good idea? But it was, she had opened up to me more than she'd opened up to anyone. We were closer than we'd ever been. My love for her surpassed where it once was.

And now I was betraying her trust.

"OK. Keep raising the money. We can do this; we have fourteen days left. I'll tell her after the next hunt."

His silence meant he didn't agree with waiting.

"OK. Speak soon."

I stared at the blank television screen. Was Sammy right? Should I just tell her now? Surely a couple of days wouldn't make much difference. It would be better if we could raise more money. But one point two million was pretty decent. It felt like the stakes were even higher now that her grandparents knew about the prize money and I knew how they wanted this as much as her. Maybe I'd grow the balls and tell her before the next hunt was over. Sammy and my dad were right. Deception was not the answer.

As I snuck back into bed Tara rolled, snuggling into me. I couldn't bear to lose her again. She'd given me the truth—she deserved the same.

THIRTEEN DAYS

Shepherd

WHEN I WOKE, Tara was in the shower. With yesterday's shower sex still fresh in my mind, I wanted to join her. Instead, I lay in bed thinking about how I would tell her about the game. Do I start with how much I missed her? Or how I remembered she loved scavenger hunts? Or maybe I should ask her how she'd feel if we didn't win?

With nothing but a towel wrapped around her, she came into the bedroom. Her long blond hair flowed down her back. Her smile made me instantly hard, but I needed to concentrate. Sitting against the headboard, I willed myself to speak.

"Good morning," she said brightly, climbing onto the bed next to me.

"Hi," was all I managed to get out before she straddled me and her lips met mine.

All reason disappeared as her wet hair brushed against my chest and she kissed me eagerly. The only thing between us was the sheet, my boxers and that damn towel hugging her body. After ripping her towel away, my hands found her breasts, kneading them. She tore her lips away from mine so she could lift herself up and yank the sheet off. I pulled down my boxers.

The gasp she let out as she slid onto me sent goose bumps across my skin. Her breasts rubbed against my chest as her mouth took mine again. Wetness increased with every rise and fall. Sex had never been this good with her before. Surely if it had, I wouldn't have waited five years. There was no way I would lose her again.

I took hold of her hips, helping her move faster as I thrust inside her. Our moans clamoured together like a hammer against a bell. With one last thrust, I came inside her, her back arching. My mouth fell upon her breasts instantly, licking both nipples one by one, increasing her tremors before she fell to the side and rested against me.

"Is that how we're going to start every morning?" I asked, still struggling to get my breath back.

"If you're up for it."

"I'm sure my dick will stand up for you any time."

Realisation slammed into me. I couldn't tell her now. Not *right* now, anyway. I couldn't say, 'Thanks for the sex, and by the way, you're here under false pretences.

Tara

"WHAT ARE our next set of clues?" I asked, leaning towards the phone and resting my hand on Shepherd's leg to steady myself.

Shepherd read the clues to me.

<u>Hunt 4</u>
Our first event was in Parramatta
over 200 years ago.
We are a not-for-profit organisation.
Our sponsors range from grand
champion to red ribbon sponsors.
In 1891, we were permitted to use
the word Royal.
We end every night with fireworks.
Oh, Candie and Ronnie, have you
seen them yet?

"That last clue is from an Elton John song, 'Bennie and the Jets,'" I said. "My parents would often sing it to us after I named my puppy, Benny. What a weird clue."

"I wonder what it means. Are we looking for Elton John?"

"Or a yellow brick road," I said.

"Maybe some sunglasses."

"Or an amazing sparkly jacket."

"The list is endless," Shepherd said, rubbing the back of his neck. "How old were you when you got Benny?"

"We got him when I was seven. The year after, we moved to the farm when my parents died. He loved it there: swimming in the dam, running to meet the school bus every afternoon, working with Pop, treats from Nan."

"It sounds like a great life for a dog."

"Sometimes he would roll in dead animals and would be

offended when he wasn't allowed inside the house. I can remember the day when he did it just before lunch time. We went inside to eat lunch. He sat at the door, barking and howling until we gave in and bathed him."

I smiled wistfully. I missed Benny. He'd been there through the toughest part of our life. He was our constant companion, and we were his. He smiled whenever he was with us and brought us joy.

"He died just before we headed off to uni. Like he knew we were going and missing us would break his heart."

I cried many nights after. The memory had me tearing up. Shepherd drew me towards him and gave my shoulders a squeeze.

"Let's figure out the rest of these clues," I said as I pulled the pad towards me.

"Do we start at the top as usual?"

"I suppose. We have an idea what the last clue means. Maybe it will make more sense as we figure out the other ones."

We scrolled through events in Parramatta and came up empty. All the events we saw were modern.

"Try adding nearly 200 years ago," I suggested.

"This site lists everything important that happened from settlement to now. Let's look for events."

He scrolled and scrolled but found nothing about events. There was so much history that I knew nothing about, like the first female orphan school built in 1818.

"Click on that," I said to Shepherd, out of curiosity.

It was a home for convict and Aboriginal girls, set up to give them a basic education and teach them how to be good domestic servants. All in a religious and moral setting to keep them from vile depravities.

"Did you read how two-thirds of them weren't orphans; they still had one living parent?" Shepherd asked.

"Yeah, mostly mothers living in poverty. And they could only see each other once a month."

"It must have been so hard for the mothers. Imagine wanting the best for your child and knowing they were being clothed and fed, but not being able to see them."

Shepherd was still as compassionate as he had always been. He may have come from money but he was kind, fair and respectful to those who worked for his family. That's where his interest in human rights came from. I looked at him to gauge his reaction. He was deep in thought.

***

Shepherd

THE FIRST TIME I'd heard about families being torn apart, our housekeeper Maria and I had been sitting on our dock on the lake, watching the fireworks. I was maybe twelve or thirteen.

When one of the neighbour's kids had been struck by a wayward firework and cried out in pain, Maria had shuddered and held me for dear life. I'd rubbed her arm trying to comfort her like she had done many times for me.

"It's OK, Maria."

I could feel her shoulders shaking, and when I looked up at her face, I saw tears streaming down her cheeks.

"I'm sorry Shepherd. It reminded me of my old home."

"Did your old home have fireworks?" I was confused, why would someone be crying because of fireworks?

"No. They had guns. That boy's cry reminded me of when people were shot."

I looked up at her, trying to process what she'd said. She gave me a sad, wistful smile.

"Where I grew up, it was not like it is here. It was not safe. We did not live in peace but rather fear. The police were corrupt, the law was corrupt, the government was corrupt."

Her eyes were far away, and I was glad that she lived with me now where she was safe.

"When I was eighteen my brother spoke out against them for falsely imprisoning people. He shouldn't have done it. He knew it would mean trouble, but he couldn't stay silent any longer while innocent people suffered.

"They were angry with him, so we went into hiding. He found a way for me and my parents to leave Mexico. As soon as he heard we were safe, he began organising protests against the government."

She looked down at me and smoothed my hair, taking a moment to catch her breath. I hung onto every word she said.

"My cousin witnessed everything that happened. He was lucky to escape with his life, but Ronaldo was not so lucky. They detained him and tortured him. They wanted him to give up his co-conspirators. He wouldn't, even through beatings, water boarding and electric shocks."

I hadn't understood what all of that meant until I googled it later. I had stared at the screen crying silent tears for a man I didn't know, but who had saved my Maria.

"These acts were done openly. And I have no doubt about what my cousin told me. When my brother and I were young, we shared a bed. Some nights, we could hear the screams of those who suffered. My parents tried to hide it from us by singing, but it could never be completely hidden.

"When they finished with Ronaldo, they hung him in the town square, leaving his body there for days as a warning and a reminder."

She took my face in her hands and held it tightly.

"I thank God every day for that brave man who gave me my freedom."

The next words she said struck me to my core, and I hoped with every ounce of my being that it was true. "I hope that as he was suffering, he could feel my loving arms around him."

From that day on I vowed to help anyone I could, but especially those who suffered at the hands of corruption.

Tara's voice interrupted my memory. "Did it say what happened to the girls?"

"It says that most girls were able to re-join their families," I read with relief.

"This clue is too hard and the not-for-profit clue is too broad," Tara said. "Let's try 'Our sponsors range from grand champion to red ribbon sponsors'."

I typed in grand champion sponsors. The fourth result showed The Sydney Royal Show.

"Do they have red ribbon sponsors, too?"

A spurt of adrenaline rushed through my body when the answer came up. "Let's see if the other clues fit as well."

Every single one of them did. We needed to go to the show. The only thing that was still not clear was the 'Benny and the Jets' clue.

"I love the show," Tara said, her smile beaming bright.

"It's like a fair. Remember the one we went to on spring break?"

"You won me a teddy on the duck shooting game. And then one on the fishing game. And then the bottle stand. I couldn't even win anything decent on the spinning wheel."

"That's what happens when you grow up in the country, you gain amazing skills."

She smiled at me and I remembered how I didn't feel embarrassed or emasculated by her prowess. In fact, it turned me on. It didn't take much then, and it still didn't.

"I still have those teddies."

Tara was about to say something but stopped before the words escaped her mouth. Her eyebrows were raised, and she looked at me quizzically.

"I never stopped loving you, Tara. I kept them as a reminder."

"I thought you would have given them to one of your party girls."

"That's all they were. Party girls. I was such a mess when you left."

This time it was my turn to be surprised. If she knew that I'd partied hard when she left, she must have been keeping an eye on me. I always thought she didn't care, so my way of coping was to pretend I didn't either. It had gone on for months before my dad had had enough. He and Sammy ambushed me one morning as I walked into the kitchen for a late breakfast.

"Sit down, son."

I looked between them, wishing I could at least grab a drink before I had to endure listening to them. Back then no hour was too early to start drinking. If I tried to have one with breakfast, Maria would confiscate it and pour it down the sink. I looked to her as she busied herself in the kitchen. She ignored me. I would get no help from her.

My dad sat opposite me and Sammy leaned his tall, lanky body against the counter.

"Shepherd, you've got to stop this nonsense. Enough is enough."

I stared at him, hoping he would just get on with it and leave.

"Tara has been gone for months. You've got to stop wallowing in self-pity."

"I'm not. I'm living life."

I glared between him and Sammy, as if daring them to tell me I was wrong.

"Come on, Shep. What happened to all the dreams you had? You were going to change the world," Sammy said.

"There's no point. Nothing I do will make a difference."

From the corner of my eye I could see Maria stiffen.

"Do you think Tara would like to see you like this?" Dad asked, trying a different tactic.

"I don't think Tara gives a shit about me or what I do."

I stood up to get a drink. Sammy strode over, his long legs carrying him quickly. He grabbed my shoulder and shoved me back into my chair. I gasped as I looked up at him, shocked; Sammy was the most non-confrontational guy I knew.

"I don't know why Tara left, but if you ever want a chance to win her back, you've got to stop this crap."

"I don't want her back," I snapped.

"Fine. Whatever. But I'm tired of this. You are a better person than this."

"Son, before Tara you were lost. She taught you so much

about yourself. Helped you find direction. Don't throw that away."

It was true. I always knew I had a purpose. I wanted to help the oppressed. Tara was the first person I told, and she supported me. We were going to do it together. Her and I against the corrupt. But she left and did it without me. How was I supposed to do it without her?

I looked between them and to Maria. I could keep fighting them or I could give in. I could make the choice to be someone Tara could be proud of. Someone they could be proud of. I could be proud of.

My dad reached out his hand and covered mine. "I'm sorry you feel lost, Shepherd. Please let us help you."

My first instinct was to shake off his hand. I considered it, but kept mine still. Sammy stood beside him. Maria had stopped busying herself, her imploring eyes closing a gap that had widened over the months. I'm certain the moment my shoulders relaxed her lips turned up at the corners, before she nodded at me and turned away.

"I don't know why she left, Dad. I thought she loved me."

"She did, son. We saw it every time she looked at you."

Sammy nodded.

"I think of her every day. I miss her."

It was true. The girls I met never measured up to Tara. They never gave me the strength she did. They were just there for a good time and I gave it to them.

"I know. But wasting your life is not the answer."

I locked eyes with Sammy and we nodded in unison.

I came out of the memory as Tara took hold of my hand, raising my downturned eyes to her, dragging myself back into her presence and lifting my slumped shoulders. I didn't want to tell her how bad it had been. It would be just another regret she would add to her list, like not telling her grandparents about Zac.

"I'm sorry, Shepherd. I'm sorry for the pain I caused you."

She climbed into my lap and held me close. I never wanted to let her go or be apart from her again.

Pulling away from her, I held her steady, pushing the hair out of her face. I kissed her as if her lips gave me life. She made me feel whole, content, like she was where I belonged.

"I love you, Shepherd."

My heart swelled. "I love you, too."

TWELVE DAYS

Tara

I WOKE UP SLOWLY, aware of Shepherd beside me. My senses took him in one by one. His leg rested against mine, spreading warmth through me. His scent lingered on the sheets. I drew the musk in, letting it settle into my lungs. His steady breathing was his own special melody. Opening my eyes, I turned my face towards his and found him looking at me, smiling.

He gave me a quick kiss and my lips were left begging for more. As he took hold of my hand he said, "Tara, I think you need to speak to your grandparents about Zac."

How long had he been thinking about this? Not six years like I had been. But it was obvious it had been weighing on him.

I stared up at the ceiling. My stomach sunk; their reaction terrified me. I was angry enough with myself for all three of us. It wasn't their anger I was scared of, though. It was their disappointment. I know that I let Zac down and I let them down. There was nothing I could do to bring him back, even if I offered my own life for his. I would do so willingly, if that were an option.

They deserved the truth. No matter what the consequences. No more hiding—six years was too long.

"You know what they say about letting sleeping dogs lie?" he asked.

"That we should leave things as they are, not to bring up the past because it can cause trouble."

"Yes. But that saying isn't always right."

"I know." Everything between Shepherd and I was out in the open. But my grandparents were a different story all together.

"What happened to Zac wasn't your fault. I know you don't believe me. Some things are not in our control, and you did everything you could."

"But did I? Maybe if I'd told my grandparents they could have saved him."

I clenched the fist of my free hand. My body was so tense it felt like a corpse in rigor mortis. Hard. Unyielding. I stared up at the ceiling.

"I'm sure you had a good reason not to."

"I didn't think it would help. Whenever I tried to speak to him it pushed him further away. I thought if they spoke to him it would push him over the edge."

Shepherd turned his face to mine. "No one can deny what you felt Tara. You were the one in the thick of it, living it every day. If that's what you thought would happen, I have no doubt it's right."

"But what if it was the wrong decision? What if it could have saved him?"

"You can second guess yourself for the rest of your life. There are a thousand what-if scenarios. None of them will bring Zac back."

I nodded. He was right, I needed to do this. I could do this. Couldn't I?

"What if my grandparents think it was the wrong decision? What if they resent me? Hate me? They're the only family I have left."

"They love you, Tara. They're proud of you, your actions, how you try to make the world a better place. But even without that, they would still be proud."

"But will they still be, after I tell them?"

"I believe they will."

I wasn't so sure. But regardless of how they might react, Shepherd was right. I needed to tell them.

Shepherd pulled me into his arms. I lay there, my resolve growing stronger. When the hunt was finished, I needed to tell my grandparents. It was something I should have done six years ago.

"I know my foundation won't bring Zac back, but I want to help so others don't have to feel my pain."

"Best we get on with the hunt then," Shepherd said, giving me a peck before getting out of bed. "We have twelve days left. We're making really good time."

Shepherd

TARA and I walked into the showgrounds hand in hand. People moved in every direction.

"This place is buzzing," I said, taking it all in.

Tara pointed at excited children tugging their parents' arms in every direction. "I don't think those parents will be letting go of their hands anytime soon. They could end up anywhere."

"Those kids are nothing like the old folk. Look, they're happy to stroll on, stopping to take everything in."

Teenagers laughed, walking fast. Farmers ambled past with a relaxed gait. Noise surrounded us but nothing was distinct. More like a constant murmur.

I checked our map. There were buildings with animals, food halls, showbag halls, rides, pavilions. It was mind boggling. Bigger than the fair Tara and I had gone to when we were at grad school. It would take us all day to look at everything, and even worse, we still didn't know what we were looking for.

"Where do you want to start?" I asked.

"I honestly don't know. Do we just walk through every section?"

"I think that's all we can do. Do you think we'll go on some rides today? Maybe the pirate ship?" I held my laugh in. I got the response I was expecting. She gave me a nudge in the ribs.

"I thought we agreed to never bring that up?"

"What, the fact that your equilibrium affected you on that day too?"

"At least I waited until I was off the ride to throw up."

I had held her hair back for her as she bent over and retched. We were laughing so hard she nearly choked. When she stood up, she took a step towards me, offering me a kiss, saying it was the least I could do seeing as I was taking advantage of her weakness. I closed my eyes, waiting with unwilling lips ready to accept my punishment. Her lips pecked my cheek instead.

"Are you done remembering every time I turned green?"

I nodded, biting my lip to stop from smiling. And then couldn't help myself. "You have to admit, it's funny that those teenagers laughed every time they saw you after that."

"You deserve a punishment kiss."

I turned my face toward her. "I guess I deserve it. Lay it on me."

Her hand reached around the back of my neck and entwined in my hair. She pulled my face towards hers. Her soft lips embraced mine. As she pulled away, she sucked lightly on my bottom lip. I breathed in deeply and opened my eyes. Damn, that was no peck on the cheek.

"Let's head this way," she said.

She led me to the closest building, which according to the map was the showbag hall. I had never seen anything like it in my life. The building was packed with people who stopped at booth after booth to see what showbags were on sale. Colourful plastic bags were attached to boards with their contents laid out beside them, set out in such a way it felt like you were getting a good deal for your dollar. There were bags for brands of chocolates that held half a dozen different bars and then a novelty toy. There were themed bags for toys. Some cost as little as two dollars and went all the way up to thirty. People walked up and down the aisles seeing what was on offer before going back to buy their bags of choice. Kids pulled on their parents' arms trying to drag them to what they wanted. Some stood wide eyed, mouths agape, staring at all the bags.

"This place is lit," I said to Tara in wonder.

"I know. It stays this busy from morning to night. Hardly anyone goes home without a showbag, even if it's just a $2 Bertie Beetle one."

Tara and I walked the aisles looking for anything that could be related to the last clue. There was nothing. No Elton John showbags, nothing about a yellow brick road, candles, crocodiles, nothing.

"Do you think we're interpreting the clue right?" Tara asked as we walked into the woodchop stadium, grabbing servings of strawberries and cream on the way.

"I have no idea. I hope when we pass whatever it is we're looking for, it jumps out at us."

"Let's sit and watch the woodchop for a while. It's a must-do at any Australian show."

The popularity of the sport was evident as the stadium seats were packed. We sat on the edge of our seat as they placed the sawn logs in their cradles. The crowd hushed as the choppers came out to stand behind their assigned logs.

"Look, there's a female chopper," Tara said, leaning in close to me.

"That's cool. Do you think she'll do well?"

"Yes. It's not all about brute strength. They need technique and fitness as well."

The contestants chipped off the ends of their logs so they would have a flat foothold. The crowd cheered for each one of them as they were announced. They were totally in the zone, practicing slow swings, thinking about where their first cuts needed to go. As they were counted in one by one according to their handicap, they began chopping. The axes hacking away at wood made a rhythmic sound. They were almost in unison. The contestants chopped left, right, left, right. The lone female competitor turned second and began chopping at the other side. Tara grasped my hand, her breath hitching. They all kept swinging, never breaking their rhythm. One by one the logs broke in half. Tara continued squeezing my hand until the female finished in third place. The crowd clapped as each competitor finished. It was mere seconds between first and last.

***

Tara

SHEPHERD and I walked around the show, keeping our eye out for the elusive treasure but getting more lost in ourselves. Holding hands and sharing smiles came naturally. When I spotted a photo booth, I couldn't resist capturing our togetherness. I pulled him towards it.

After we put our money in the slot, we hopped into the booth, pulling the curtain closed behind us. The noise from the rides, and the constant chiming and loud calls from the vendors in sideshow alley disappeared. We did some standard couple shots before pulling crazy faces. With two photos to go, Shepherd pulled me into his lap and kissed me deeply.

His mouth moved with such intensity I was lost in him. Strawberries and cream tantalised my taste buds. His warm hand found its way under my shirt, resting on my back. Heat radiated from his palm and through my body, settling in my core. I changed position so I could straddle him, bringing us closer. His hardness pressed against me and I became wet in response.

His hands found my breasts. I sighed into his mouth. I braced myself against the warm metal of our enclosure as Shepherd suckled on my neck. I pushed against him. Feeling his dick pressed between my legs wasn't nearly enough. The warm air surrounding us was heated further by our burning need for each other. Shepherd's heavy breathing sparked something deep inside of me.

"Shepherd," I breathed out, sinking lower onto him.

A loud knock banged on the side of the booth.

"Are you finished in there?" a male voice called out.

I jumped; my heart crashed against my ribcage.

"Yes," I said in a voice too high to sound natural.

I hopped off Shepherd so quickly I almost fell over. My hand pushed against the curtain, which gave me no purchase. Shepherd took hold of my waist, steadying me.

"Sorry, one sec," I called out.

Straightening my clothing, I tried to look respectable as I left the photo booth with Shepherd close behind, letting out a chuckle. I felt like a horny teenager getting caught in a compromising position.

We made it three steps before the man spoke again. "Don't you want these?"

I turned to see him holding our photos. Striding back to him, I took the photos before returning to Shepherd's side. He put his arm around my shoulder and pulled me in close to settle a kiss on top of my head.

"I look forward to finishing that off later."

Heat surged through me all over again as we continued walking hand in hand to the show ring. We watched some dogs who were being judged. They were pointers.

"Maybe the clue is about my dog, Benny. Maybe we need

to be looking for a pointer."

"That might be it. Let's head into the pavilions," Shepherd said, pulling me to a doorway.

This could be what we were looking for. It made sense. But did it?

"How would the organiser know about Benny though? And how would the other teams know it was about a pointer?"

Shepherd shrugged. "The organisers would have done their research. And maybe the other teams' clues aren't exactly the same as ours."

"That doesn't seem fair to have different playing fields for everyone."

Shepherd didn't say anything as we walked past cubicle after cubicle of pointers. Most of them were fast asleep. I looked at each dog closely for a resemblance of Benny while Shepherd looked at the names. I didn't know how the organiser would know that Benny existed, let alone what he looked like, but I was leaving no stone unturned.

"Hello," a middle-aged man with salt and pepper hair said as we stopped by his cubicle.

"Hi. The dogs look tuckered out, they must have had a big day," I said.

"Sometimes it's hard work doing nothing."

Shepherd stood beside me. "How do dog shows work exactly?"

"We start with training the dog to move a certain way. And we teach them about grooming when they're young, so they learn what to expect. They need to look their best for the judges."

The man looked at Shepherd, who nodded.

"We go into the ring and do some exercises as requested

by the judge – up and back, in a triangle and a circle. Some-times individually, sometimes in a group."

"Why all of those?" Shepherd asked.

"They are checking conformation and movement. Then they judge them up close to see how they fit into what is expected of the breed – coat, bones, stature. That sort of thing."

I left Shepherd with the man and continued looking at the dogs. While they all looked similar to Benny, none had his rich chocolate colour. I stopped in my tracks when I found one named Benny. He was fast asleep. I scanned the area trying to see if the owner was nearby. No one was there. I stepped closer to the dog to see if I could find any treasure. The dog stirred as I approached but did not move his head. Shepherd and the man moved towards us.

Shepherd

"YOUR MAN here tells me you're looking for a dog. Some-thing about a scavenger hunt?"

"Yes. I think this is the one. When I was younger, I had a pointer named Benny."

"And what exactly do you think the treasure is?"

"I don't know. I can't see anything that stands out."

The man stepped behind the rope and approached the dog cage. He trailed his fingers across the metal. I tensed, hoping he wasn't going to wake the dog. I didn't want it to wake up without its owner there. Bending down, he reached for something before standing, brandishing an envelope.

"We owners talk, you know. We've been expecting you."

I thanked him as he handed over the envelope. He watched us closely as we opened it and read the card inside. It was a puppy adoption certificate. Tara's wide eyes turned to me as she stepped away, handing me the card.

"I can't have a dog."

Not *we* can't have a dog.

"I don't have a yard and I don't have time. What if I decide I want to go overseas?"

She stepped further away from me.

"Whoa, slow down lass," the man said. "You don't have to take a dog. It was just an offer. And it doesn't need to be now; it's for when you're ready."

Tara still looked startled.

"If I were to get a dog, I would want to get a homeless one. There are too many unwanted pets in Australia."

"That's no worries, love. We have rescue pointers too."

As we walked away, Tara said, "I'm still not sure how the organisers know about Benny. He died years ago."

Now was the time to tell her. It was the perfect opportunity. But the way she stepped away from me, and how she said she might want to go overseas, made me feel a little less confident about where we were at. About how secure our relationship was.

"Well, we're talking about millions of dollars. I'm sure their research was thorough."

"I suppose. It's a bit irresponsible, buying a pet for someone, though."

"I don't think they would just let you have a dog. He was very intent on making sure they got the best owners."

We hopped into the hotel's lift, Tara's hand resting on my

leg as she pushed herself against me. As she leant closer to whisper in my ear, her hand made its way up my thigh, enticingly close to my crotch. My dick strained toward her.

"Are you ready to finish what we started?" Her breath was warm against my ear. My dick grew even more. And my doubt disappeared.

Spinning her around so her back was towards me, I pushed my hardness into her. I held her close as I kissed the back of her neck, listening to her breath hitch. "Readier than you'll ever be."

The doors slid open and a lady entered with her beagle. Tara pushed herself against me so her butt rubbed against my dick. She grasped my testicles giving them a rub and squeeze. In alarm, I looked toward the lady. But she wouldn't have been able to see anything; Tara's body covered that delicate part. Then Tara stepped forward and introduced herself to the dog, leaving me stranded against the back wall trying to adjust my hard on so it didn't greet everyone who stepped into the lift. I grinned to myself. I would need to make her pay for that.

The doors opened at our floor and Tara threw a smile back to me as she got out. I didn't take my eyes off her pretty arse until we reached the door to our apartment.

Tara

THE DOOR HADN'T EVEN CLOSED behind us before Shepherd shoved me against it. The desire in his eyes made my core burn., and his mouth met mine as his body pushed against me. He didn't even bother undoing my jeans, his hand just found its way between my legs and rubbed. A bolt of electricity shot through me as my mouth opened to his. I yanked his t-shirt off in desperation to feel his smooth skin. Just the feel of it sent me another notch closer to coming in my pants.

Ripping my shirt and bra off he pinned me tightly against the door, before making room for his hand to grab my breast. I moaned into his mouth, the sound coming from deep within. I wanted him to take my jeans off and have me right there, but Shepherd had other ideas. He took a breast in his mouth, sucking and rolling his tongue around my nipple. My back arched as he continued rubbing between my legs. I took hold of his shoulders, pushing against them, moaning his name as my panties soaked through. I didn't want to come right there. But it felt so good, I didn't want it to stop either.

Shepherd reached down and undid my jeans, pulling them and my underwear down. I stepped out of them with jerky movements, trying not to fall over in the process. His mouth made its way down my body, sending uncontrolled pulses of lust through me. As his fingers plunged into me, his mouth was there licking and sucking. He threw my leg over his shoulder to gain better access. With each suck and lick the tension inside me grew. I stood on the tips of my toes, trying to distance myself from his tongue and slow down my response. Shepherd's strong hands held me firm. Coils of pleasure rushed through me as the pressure inside me released in waves. I orgasmed around his fingers. My legs gave way and his fingers sank further in. I'm sure they were the only thing holding me up.

As his lips made their way back to my mouth, his fingers slipped out. I could feel their wetness, my wetness, as he took hold of me, pulling me closer to him. My legs continued to shake. I should return the favour but I couldn't move.

Shepherd carried me to the bedroom. As soon as my back hit the bed, he plunged into me and the pleasure started all over again.

I wanted Shepherd every day for the rest of my life. The way he made me feel alive and wanted, matched with his gentleness and kindness, made him perfect. He never made me feel like I was weak, yet he strengthened me in ways he would never know. But he should know. I needed to tell him how much he meant to me.

Shepherd

AS I LAY beside Tara regaining my breath and some sort of composure, I promised myself I would never live another day without her.

As usual, when I had been close to telling her about the hunt, I chickened out. We were close to being found out anyway with that stunt Sammy had pulled with the dog. What was he thinking?

After Tara fell asleep, I walked into the lounge room so I could call him. I needed to know how the fundraising was going. It felt stupid and weak for a dollar figure to hold me back from telling Tara, but it wasn't the money. I was scared. She had left me once before without even a word and I hadn't done anything wrong—that I knew about at the time. This time she would have a reason. And I wasn't convinced she was in this for the long haul. While I had no fear about talking about us or our future, she was nowhere near talking about those things yet.

"Hi, Shepherd," Sammy said as he answered the phone.

"Hi, Sammy."

"Have you told Tara yet?"

"Have you raised the money yet?"

I knew I was being stubborn and immature. Seconds of silence ensued.

"Shepherd—"

"Yeah, I know. Sorry."

If I couldn't talk to Sammy about it, who could I talk to? I went out to the balcony. The cold air hit me, waking up my tired brain.

"I'm scared, Sammy. I don't think she's as committed as I am."

"You can't hide forever, Shep. It's better to find out now."

"But if I give it a bit more time—"

"Shep, enough. You need to tell her."

"Yeah. OK. How is the fundraising going?"

"We're at a standstill now. They're asking questions I can't answer, about the foundation, how the money will be used."

"Have you asked everyone from the list I gave you?"

"Yes, and some of my contacts as well. We're up to one point five million."

"She is relying on this money. I need to get it for her."

I gripped the railing tightly. This was nothing like I expected it to be. All I wanted to do was come here, have fun in the fake scavenger hunt and convince Tara to give me a second chance. Clenching my teeth, I shook my head. I wanted to kick something. I needed to go for a run or something to clear my head.

"Has she told you why she left yet?"

I told him everything. The more I spoke the more dread filled my stomach. She didn't trust me enough before and now it felt like I was betraying the trust she did have in me. Twelve days. We had twelve days to raise the rest of the money.

"It'll be OK. She will see you had your heart in the right place."

I wasn't as convinced. After I hung up with Sammy, I went into the bedroom. Tara was fast asleep. I pulled on some shorts, tank top and sneakers and headed down to the gym. I ran until sweat was dripping off me and my legs were ready to give out. The whole time I ran, I thought about how I could get the extra $1.5 million. I was out of options. My next trust payment wouldn't come in soon enough. And even if it did, it wouldn't come close to covering what we needed. It's not like I could crowd fund—that method should only be used for people in great need. And my fuck up didn't qualify as a great need.

The only answer was to grow some balls and tell Tara the truth. Before the twelve days were up.

Tara stirred when I entered the room. "Where have you been?"

"I went for a run. I needed to think."

Her eyes became more alert although her prone body said otherwise. "What about?"

"I'll tell you later. I need a shower."

Fucking hell, Shepherd. You're such a dick.

ELEVEN DAYS

Tara

WAKING up to Shepherd was the best part of my day. I couldn't believe we were lucky enough to have a second chance. I listened to his slow breathing. It was different to last night when he had gone for a run.

Something must be bothering him for him to go for a run like that. Would he be able to open up and tell me what it was? We spoke about some of the things we did in those five years apart. But it was nothing deep. We didn't talk about our relationship or how we felt. Was he holding back, on purpose, because he didn't want to share those things? It was nothing definitive, just a feeling.

I must be reading too much into it. He was tired just like I was. That's probably all it was.

Shepherd's phone beeped beside him. He reached out for it and read the message. Rolling over he saw I was awake and handed the phone to me.

Congratulations. You've earned a day off.

"A day off? In the middle of a competition? That's a bit weird."

"I'll say." His voice sounded strange, deflated, monotone. What was going on with him? I thought he would have said how great it was.

"I don't know what we could possibly do all day." I rolled on top of him. I sucked on his neck and kissed his stubbled jaw before finding his soft lips. His kiss was slow, tender. He was hard in an instant and the knowledge that it was his reaction to me caused lust to swell in my body. My lips went to his collar bone and down to his chest. The softness and warmth of his skin excited me nearly as much as his hard on. My lips drifted down further.

His sharp intake of breath made my lust swell. He pulled me back up to his lips and rolled me over, so he was on top of me, controlling the intensity. Wrapping my fingers around the back of his neck I caressed his hair. The longing between my legs didn't change but I fell into his trance.

His lips found my neck and his hand my breast. Without me even knowing it happened we were both naked, lying skin to skin. I could feel him between my legs, and I was almost begging him to enter me. He was content with kissing and exploring my body. When I thought the untamed desire would overtake me, he slid in with long, languid strokes. All the times we'd had sex in the last few days was nothing like this. Those had been all passion. This was about desire and a need of a different kind. I wanted to tell him I felt it too. That he filled me completely.

"Shepherd—"

He cut me off with a kiss that kept rhythm with his strokes. His breath quickened and his lips left mine. His breath whispered against my neck: the catch and exhale. In response my skin tingled, each gasp awakened the nerves. I moved my hips so he went deeper, right to my core. A rush of pleasure radiated from where he drove into me. Holding each other tight, we went over the edge together, our orgasms like waves crashing until they petered out, caressing the shore. We held each other until the last pulse dissipated.

Shepherd rolled off me and we both stared up at the ceiling, unable or unwilling to speak.

I didn't know if sex with him could be any better.

***

Shepherd

I'D NEVER EXPERIENCED anything like that in my life and I doubted I ever would again. And as we lay beside each other connected by our hands, I felt that our togetherness would last through the ages. That if we were the only two people left in the world, I would never tire of her.

Did she feel the same? I wanted to ask her, but I was afraid of what I didn't want to hear. That this was a short-term thing for her. But that was stupid. Why would she share her past with me if she saw no future? Would she see a future once she found out about the hunt? And about the three million dollars that didn't exist, decimating her chance to honour her brother?

"What do you want to do today?" I asked, turning my head to hers.

"I'm not fussed." She continued to stare up at the ceiling. "We could have a lazy morning and watch a movie in bed."

"Sounds good. Maybe this afternoon we could go for a walk along the harbour and have dinner somewhere."

"Like a date?"

What was that in her voice? Surprise? Discomfort?

My heart dropped.

"Yeah, stupid idea."

She turned her face to mine. "Shepherd, I didn't say it was a stupid idea. I was just surprised."

"It doesn't matter. We probably don't have enough money anyway."

"I think it's a good idea. It would be nice to do something away from the hunt."

I sat up and swung my legs off the bed. I didn't believe that's what she really wanted. I didn't believe anything anymore. But that was unfair. Just because I was hiding the truth, it didn't mean she was. The guilt was weighing on me so much that I was finding blame where there was no blame to lay. It was all my fault and my weakness and lie only multiplied any doubt I had.

Sitting up beside me, she said, "What were you thinking about last night? When you went for a run?"

That simple comment about the dog had thrown everything. And the three-million-dollar lie crashed down onto my head. If she wanted to go overseas three million dollars wouldn't make her stay. "I'm having a shower. Then I'm going to look at our expenditure to see if we can make it to the end. You can watch a movie if you like."

When I got out of the shower Tara's voice drifted in from the other room. I could barely hear it. I walked to the bedroom door so I could hear better.

"How's the competition going?" her nan asked.

"Good. We've got one hunt left to go."

"That's good timing. You'll have a few days to spare. It will be nice to spend them with Shepherd."

"Yeah." She didn't sound very enthused by it at all.

"What's wrong, Tara?" her pop asked.

Tara's voice got further away as she walked to her room. I leant against the door, trying to hear.

"Nothing. I don't know."

"Have you spoken to Shepherd about why you left?"

"Yes."

"And?"

"I don't know. He acted like he understood."

"What do you mean acted?"

Exactly. What did she mean? I *did* understand.

"He was nice, himself...it just doesn't seem right."

My stomach clenched and a pain pierced my heart. Those words confirmed what I'd feared. She didn't feel the same as I did. I strained to hear more, but couldn't hear clearly without moving closer. Some words filtered in but I discerned more mumbling and silence than anything else.

"I'm not ready...."

"Give it a chance..."

"It's not the same...I can't...it's too hard."

"Winning...top of my agenda..."

"Three million..."

Three million dollars was at the top of her agenda. Money I didn't have.

I didn't need to hear anymore. I got dressed and sat on the edge of my bed. My head felt heavy. My heart felt heavy.

It was a mistake. The whole thing was a mistake. I shouldn't have come here.

Tara

THE BED MOVED as Shepherd got up. I watched him through half closed eyes as he put his running gear on and left.

Running again? In the middle of the night? Why? He'd been standoffish all day. He had looked at figures, and was lost in scrolling on his phone. After dinner, he took himself to bed and hadn't acknowledged me when I lay down next to him.

I stared up at the ceiling while I waited for him to come back and replayed the phone call with my grandparents over in my head.

"It just doesn't seem right."

"Tara, sweetie, what do you mean?" Nan asked.

"I don't know. We never discuss anything about our future."

I sat on the bed, pulling at the red throw. My fingers clutched, lifted, let go.

"You've only been together for a few days after spending five years apart. You can't just pick up where you left off."

"Yeah, I suppose." I flopped down onto the bed and stared at the white ceiling.

"Have you brought up the subject?" Pop asked.

"I'm not ready."

"Maybe Shepherd is feeling the same. Give it a chance."

That was true. Why did I expect him to talk about it when I wasn't even ready?

"Maybe he's trying to rebuild trust in you. Maybe he

wants to be sure you're not going to leave before he opens himself up."

I had swallowed the lump down in my throat. My stupidity in running away had caused all this. If I'd just stayed five years ago and spoken to him, we wouldn't be here now. He would have either quit being a party boy before he even started or he would have broken my heart by ignoring my fears. I honestly doubted the second option.

"What if it's too hard for him to ever trust me again?"

"Tara, sweetie, love has a way of forgiving even when we think it's impossible."

I hoped so because I loved Shepherd more than words could say. Life without him all over again would feel like death.

"How's the hunt going?" Pop asked.

"Good. We're nearly done. I'm not sure winning is at the top of my agenda anymore."

"What is then?"

"Shepherd. Sure, the three million dollars would be great. But if we don't win, knowing I have him would be enough. I would find another way to help people."

I heard the door open and glanced at the clock. Shepherd had been gone for over an hour. Something must be really bothering him. Was he finding it too hard to be with me? Now that he had gotten the explanation that he'd been waiting for, did his feelings fall flat? What if I was ready to give him my life and he didn't want it? But he couldn't tell me, so he was running to ease his suffering and his inability to escape.

I needed to ask.

Shepherd

I LAY DOWN NEXT to Tara after my shower. The tenseness and sadness had not left me. I spent half the time away from the room googling ideas on how to raise the extra money. I was out of options. There was nothing I could do in the ten days we had left. Nothing that could net me one and a half million dollars. So, I ran. I could run until my legs stopped moving but I couldn't outrun those words:

'I'm not ready. It's too hard.'

Followed by 'The top of my agenda...three million dollars.'

And then Sammy's words echoed in my head, "We're at a standstill."

Tara not being ready. Three million dollars not being ready. And I wasn't ready to tell her that this hunt was all made up.

TEN DAYS

Tara

SHEPHERD WAS dead to the world next to me. That run must have really taken it out of him. I had a swag of questions for him but would I be brave enough to ask him when he woke, starting with what was bothering him? My mind was running at a hundred miles an hour, going around and around in circles, like it was racing in the Indy 500. Was it something to do with our last hunt? He was perfectly fine until then. What had happened on the hunt? What? I don't know. It was just a dog. And a certificate for a puppy. Why would he be weirded out by that?

I lay still beside him until he stirred. Every morning he would roll over and give me a smile. Today, instead, he swung his legs out of bed and declared, "I'm going for a run."

I held back my tears. Could he not stand looking at me that much? It didn't make sense. Nothing made sense.

Getting changed, he didn't even spare a glance in my

direction. It was one thing to break the rules at night, but during the day?

"Do you think that's a good idea? Aren't we supposed to stay together?"

His shoulders tensed. He still didn't look at me. "You can come if you like.'

The harshness in his voice was like a slap to the face. "You can send a text to see if it's OK if you prefer."

He grabbed the phone off the bedside table and texted. My eyes stung.

He read the return text and threw the phone onto the bed. "Looks like you'll have to come with me."

He still didn't look at me. I knew when I wasn't wanted, but I had no choice now, did I? I got changed and followed him to the lift. He stood on the opposite side and watched the floor numbers tick down, not once acknowledging my presence.

I bit the inside of my cheek taking attention away from the pain in my heart. It was less than forty-eight hours ago when we had been in the same lift barely able to keep our hands off each other.

He hopped on a treadmill and ran while I rode a bike, each of us lost in our own thoughts. I stopped after five km, but Shepherd ran and ran. And I sat and waited, trying to figure out what was going on in his mind as the minutes ticked by. When he finished the sweat was pouring off him.

Just ask. Just ask, I kept saying to myself. It was stupid, I needed to ask. Otherwise what did that say about us? About our relationship?

We walked to the lift in silence. As the lift rose, I built up the courage. "Shepherd, what's wrong?"

"Nothing."

"Really?"

"I don't want to talk about it."

Silence surrounded us. We separated inside our apartment door and went to our own bathrooms to shower. My heart felt like it had been pulled out of my chest, dropped onto the ground and stomped on. My tears mixed with the water. What was going on?

Shepherd was in the kitchen making breakfast when I walked out of my room. I stood at the end of the bench, to the side, so my body wasn't confrontational.

"Are you ready to talk about it?"

He continued whisking the eggs before adding some milk. His mouth twisted in a grimace. "You don't think of us as a couple, do you?"

A couple? "What?"

"What are we, Tara? Just a couple of people who have hooked up and will go our separate ways after the competition? After you get your three million dollars?"

Is that what he thought we were? I hoped we were more than that.

"I don't know. What do you think we are?"

"If you can't answer that simple question, it's obvious to me we aren't much."

He turned away and put the eggs in the pan. He stood at the stove and watched the eggs without his usual attention. They cooked quickly and were ready before the bacon and toast.

"Shepherd, we haven't even spoken about it. I don't know what you want."

"Damn it, Tara. I want you. I've always wanted you. But you don't feel the same, do you?"

I reeled at his abruptness and anger.

"I do feel the same." My voice sounded small even to my own ears.

"Really? Is that why you'd go overseas again without giving me a second thought? Is that why you told your grandparents it's too hard? That you can't do this?"

He dished breakfast up and shoved my plate towards me.

"What are you talking about? I'm not going anywhere."

"You said it yourself, you don't want a puppy because you might want to go overseas again. Is that why you don't want me?"

Tears sprung into my eyes. "I do want you."

"It sure as hell doesn't feel like it. You even told your grandparents you can't do this. I would do anything for you Tara. I even organised—"

He stopped abruptly, strode to his room and slammed the door.

<hr>

Shepherd

I WASN'T GOING to tell her I'd organised the hunt to win her back. Not now that I knew how she felt. I felt stupid enough without saying it out loud.

Arrgghh. I couldn't even face my worst fear. Instead I deflected it onto Tara. The look on her face when I unloaded onto her will haunt me for the rest of my life. She did well to hold back the threatening tears.

But I will also remember that small unconvincing voice that said, 'I do want you'. That voice will never leave me. I wanted to throw up. We had one more hunt to get through and then I'd disappear. I knew her answer now. It—this—was pointless.

She was here for three million dollars and that's what I'd give her.

I texted Sammy.

Hurry up with the next set of clues. I need this to be over.

Minutes ticked by. I imagined Sammy waking up and looking at the phone, bewildered.

Shep, what's going on?

She doesn't love me. She never did. She's just here for the money.

Three dots appeared on the screen.

Ask Dad for the rest of the money. Tell him I'll pay him back.

A few trust payments would cover it, I guess. And I could cut my salary. What a mess. I don't know how I ever thought this was a good idea. What was I even thinking?

Have you told her?

There's no point.

I'm coming down there. I'll catch the next flight.

Don't bother.

Three dots again.

Let me do this last thing for her.

Shepherd, you're not being rational.

The truth was I was never rational when it came to Tara.

Sammy, just send the clues. When we're done, make up some reason to end the competition sooner. I can't take another ten days!

I wouldn't give her the chance to run this time. No, this time, I would do it for her. I would get her what she came here for; that was only fair. I hope Dad had the money.

My throat ached from trying to keep the tears in. She didn't argue. She didn't even say that she loved me or that she wanted to stay with me. As much as it hurt, I knew it was better this way. I could stop wondering, hoping. I'd lost five years of my life wanting to be with her. She didn't feel the same.

And if I told her now about the hunt, she would crucify me. Not only had I lied to her, I'd wasted her time. I'd dragged her from her life under false pretences. The one consolation would be her having the money. And that would be here soon.

I didn't want to stop her from going overseas if that's what she wanted. Not out of guilt for me raising three million dollars for her. I wanted her to be happy, to live her dreams, even if that was without me.

I sat on my bed, put my head in my hands and cried.

Tara

I THREW the food in the bin and washed the dishes. I couldn't eat.

What was happening?

I didn't want to leave Shepherd. I was happy with him. Happier than I had been in a long time. Had I not told him that? Maybe not. But surely, Shepherd knew I loved him, especially after I shared everything with him. Being here wasn't about the money anymore. Shepherd was my future. He was what I needed.

I sat on the lounge chair and waited.

Finally, the door clicked open and my stomach lurched. Shepherd's eyes were red. I stood up so I could go to him, to help him fight whatever demons were haunting him. I needed to tell him he misheard the conversation with my grandparents.

"Shep—"

"We have our next set of clues." His voice held a melancholy tone I'd never heard from him before.

"Shepherd, we need to talk."

"About the hunt only. Remember? Your rules. Let's look at the clues."

"Shepherd, I don't know what you heard but—"

"The clues, Tara."

OK. He obviously wasn't ready to talk. I'd wait it out, but not forever. I felt like smacking him over the head but clenched my fists by my side instead.

I sat with him at the table. I wanted to reach out for his hand, to touch him, to reassure him I was there for him. Or I could take his face in my hands and kiss him until all the hurt was washed away. Instead I sat stiff and awkward. It was even more awkward than it had been in those first few days. Our bodies were not turned into each other. My hands were pressed between my legs. I didn't feel free to touch him. I was too afraid of what he might do, of his reaction.

He read the clues out to me.

Hunt 5

**Walk through alleys and cobbled
streets.
This was a slum and was going to be
demolished.
A shark ate a shark ate an arm.
Stars cannot be blotted out by the
city lights.
Enjoy 285ml of amber liquid.**

"The clues don't get any easier," I said, trying to make conversation.

"We'll figure it out. Hopefully, you will get the money for your foundation. It will all be worth it then."

"What do you mean, it will all be worth it, then?"

"All of this, being away from our jobs and lives. If you get the money it will feel like it's not a waste."

My stomach twisted. *Not a waste?* Did he think finding each other again was a *waste?* Was this even Shepherd talking? He sounded nothing like the Shepherd I knew; I'd never seen him bitter or withdrawn. Had I done this to him?

"I don't think it's been a waste at all."

He ended the conversation by typing a clue into the computer.

Shepherd

I COULDN'T BE BOTHERED WORKING out the clues. I wished Sammy had just given me the answer so I could direct us to the treasure quicker. Being this close to Tara, knowing she didn't feel the same as I did, was devastating. Tears would sprout and I would run my tongue across the top of my mouth to stop them.

She leaned closer as we looked at the results for the alley ways and cobblestones clue. It took all of my power to not move away. It took equally as much power not to kiss her.

"Could we really get that lucky and get a hit on the first clue?" she asked, as The Rocks came up with photos of alleyways and cobblestones.

I bit my tongue as my feelings fought with each other. Relief and disappointment.

She looked at me for a reaction, then continued, "Let's see if the other clues fit into The Rocks."

I shifted in my seat as I read that The Rocks were indeed regarded as a slum. The houses were decrepit and the area had been frequented by sailors and prostitutes. It had even had a breakout of the Bubonic Plague. We scrolled through pages of ramshackle homes and decaying siding. The whole area was to be torn down and rebuilt, until protestors put a stop to it.

I typed in *the rocks a shark ate a shark*. My eyes widened as a result titled '*shark arm murder*' popped up. I looked at Tara, whose wide eyes stared back as she grabbed my arm. My skin heated at her touch. I pulled away, covering my act by reaching for my drink.

"Can you believe what we're reading?" I asked.

A man who was out fishing caught a shark and decided to put it in a pool at his aquarium. A few days later the shark got sick and vomited up a human arm. Apparently, a small shark had swallowed the arm and then the big shark swallowed the small shark. An investigation ensued and a tattoo on the arm was identified. On the morning of the trial the lead witness was shot dead at The Rocks. The Rocks. This clue led directly to there.

"What about the other clue about stars not being blotted out by city lights?" she asked.

I checked my notebook to confirm the clue. "I don't know. It doesn't make sense. The Rocks is right on the edge of the city."

We typed in the clue and got no hits.

"When we looked at the clues for the Botanic Gardens, the Observatory came up as one of the options. That's near The Rocks, isn't it?"

My heart skipped a beat. "Yes."

"And if you look through a telescope, the city lights won't block anything out."

I nodded. "That's true."

"The Rocks must be the answer. Type in the last clue."

I typed in *The Rocks 285ml.*

I did and scrolled until Tara grabbed my wrist.

"Shepherd, stop. Look, a pub tour."

"What's that got to do with it?"

"Glasses hold 285ml. Amber liquid is Australian for beer. We must have to go on a pub tour."

Without a conscious effort, my hand turned over so it could hold Tara's. Her fingers moved lightly against my skin. I jerked my hand away. I couldn't afford to fall for how natural everything felt with her.

"I'll make the booking."

AS WE WALKED through the laneways from pub to pub I was continually drawn back to Tara. Even if I walked away to the other side of the group, before I knew it, I was beside her again. I shoved my hands in my pockets to stop them from reaching for hers. My stomach sunk whenever I got close to her. I needed this game to end. My heart was breaking over and over again. I couldn't take ten more days of this.

"Your boyfriend can't stay away from you," a young lady said to Tara.

"He's not my boyfriend. He's—"

I felt like I'd been punched and my head was reeling on my shoulders.

I didn't wait for the rest of the statement. I drifted to the back of the group, out of earshot.

Tara

THE YOUNG LADY looked at me with a wistful smile. "I hope I can say that about someone someday, that they are the love of my life."

"I hope so too." I looked around for Shepherd. He was at the back of the group. When I made eye contact with him his eyes darted away. Biting my lip, I turned my attention back to the tour guide.

I wish Shepherd would give me a chance to explain. Every time I tried to bring up the subject of the phone call, he brushed me off by walking away. If he would just *listen*, even for one minute, he would see that he had the wrong end of the stick. I tried not to pressure him while he was being so reactive. I needed to give him time to calm down, choose my moment. There was still time. The competition was not going to end for ten more days.

At the last pub, the barman set down coasters before handing us our beers. My coaster was different to everyone else's. It was green, and in white, bold writing it said, 'Shepherd & Tara'. On the back was written *Aletheuontes de en Agape*. What did that even mean? Maybe it was the pub's motto.

This was it. It was our last treasure.

I held it up to show Shepherd. His sad smile reflected his mood.

As we walked back to the apartment Shepherd was silent, looking down at the footpath. In the lift, he didn't utter a word, he just stared ahead. And when we got to the apartment, he paused inside the apartment door. I turned to face him. As he moved towards me, looking down at my face, my heart fluttered. His hand reached out and cupped the back of my head. My lips parted waiting for his.

They were left waiting.

Shepherd kissed my forehead. "Goodnight, Tara."

I watched him walk to his room and shut the door.

Sighing, I turned away. I needed to make this better. I needed him to know how much I loved him.

NINE DAYS

Tara

THERE WAS a persistent knocking on the apartment door. I rolled over, half asleep, wondering if Shepherd was going to answer it. When I heard no movement from his side of the apartment, I got up.

Standing outside was a tall man. A man I recognised instantly.

"Sammy?"

"Hi, Tara."

"What are you doing here?"

"Where's Shepherd?"

"In his room. Is something wrong?"

Sammy followed the direction of my eyes and strode over to the closed door.

"Yes. I've had enough of the two of you. I'm here to sort it out once and for all."

"Sort what out?"

Sammy barged into Shepherd's room and stopped dead just inside the threshold.

My heart thumped as ice pumped through my veins. I walked towards him, dread filling me more with each step. Sammy's face turned white. "It's too late."

My heart beat faster than I ever thought possible. Spots played in my vision.

"He's gone."

The ice in my veins turned to burning liquid. I pushed past Sammy, trying to gasp in enough air to keep me upright.

The room was empty. There was no sign of Shepherd or his belongings. My legs were numb. Sammy grabbed me by the elbow and directed me towards the lounge, settling me into a chair. He sat opposite me, shaking his head. My heart was slowing down. As the shock cleared, my mind cleared.

"Sammy, what are you doing here? How did you know where Shepherd was?'

His hands raked through his hair. It was such a Shepherd move. They were so alike and yet polar opposites in some ways. Slumping his shoulders, he rested his elbows on his knees and looked down at his feet.

"Sammy?"

"There is no scavenger hunt competition, Tara. It was all made up."

"What do you mean *made up*?"

Shepherd

SITTING IN THE AIRLINE LOUNGE, I scrolled through my photos. Tears stung my eyes. I turned my phone off and put it in my bag. They were memories now. They needed to stay that way. Looking at them, thinking about her, was not going to change anything.

As soon as Sammy had told me he had the three million and was ready to transfer it to Tara's account, I knew it was time to leave. There was no point staying any longer. I would only be torturing myself. I couldn't tell her I'd made up the game.

I asked her to be honest and open with her grandparents and yet I couldn't do the same thing with her. Fear held her back. Fear held me back. How was it fair to consider my fear greater than hers? I was such a fucking hypocrite.

The time we'd spent together, before I'd learned the truth, would be held close to my heart for the rest of my days. When I had thought she loved me in return, I had felt complete, that nothing would ever be able to bring me down. I should have known better. I had felt like that five years ago. She destroyed me then and here we were again.

I needed to get home, to get back to work and distract myself. I would work sixteen hours a day if I needed to, if it would keep her off my mind. Dad couldn't go through what I did last time. There would be no drowning in my sorrows, no sleeping around. It would just be work.

But different work. No more work for corporations—I wanted to do something more important. I thought I needed Tara to make that happen, but now I knew that wasn't true. I was a good person and I could do good things. Sure, having

Tara with me would be a dream come true. That wasn't going to happen; I needed to be my best self without her by my side.

I pulled my laptop out and logged into my work emails. Now was as good a time as any to get back to the grindstone.

I needed to be satisfied with the knowledge she had enough money to start her foundation. That's what she was in the game for. If nothing else, I gave her that.

Tara

SAMMY'S EYES MET MINE. He sighed.

How could the scavenger hunt be made up? There were clues that came by text and treasures we found...and rules that forced us together every moment of every day, and Shepherd being my partner.

"Best you start explaining, Sammy."

He sighed again.

"When you left, Shepherd was destroyed. I've never seen anyone sink so low. He started drinking and using drugs, but the alcohol was what stuck. And trust me, that was bad enough. The only time he didn't drink was when he was asleep or when he was working. Tara, I don't think you understand how bad it was. His dad and I thought we were going to lose him."

"I thought he was just partying."

"That's the problem with you two. You were watching him from afar and he was doing the same with you. He watched you take on the life you both dreamed of. Without him. And then you started seeing that doctor."

I shifted in my seat. I didn't think Shepherd even cared about me. All I saw were photos of him with a different girl every other week. He saw me with Emilio. Oh God, I knew what it felt like when I saw him with all those girls. It would have been a million times worse if he was serious about any of them, like Emilio and I were.

"All those girls—"

"All those girls were his weak arsed attempt to drive you from his mind. The alcohol wouldn't do it. It wouldn't numb him enough. So, he tried to fill the emptiness with more emptiness."

Sammy kept talking, telling me every last detail about how Shepherd broke—shattered might be a better word. Oh God, poor Shepherd. I'd tried to protect myself and in return I'd destroyed him. The person I loved most in the world. The person who, for twelve months, showed me nothing but devotion. He shared his dreams with me, dreams he held back from everyone else in his life. And what did I do? With one rash decision, I threw that devotion away and virtually stole his dreams.

I apologised days ago for the pain I caused. That apology now felt shallow. I'd no idea what he'd truly experienced.

My heart twisted painfully as the tears rolled down my cheeks.

Sammy watched me silently. He moved as if to get up, but changed his mind.

I didn't think I could listen any more. I knew I'd caused him pain. But if I had really listened to his words a few days ago, I would have understood the intensity of it.

Even a week ago I could have told myself what I did was OK. It was OK to protect myself. That it made perfect sense.

For five years I'd lived with my heartbreak by telling myself there was nothing else I could do. But that wasn't true, was it?

"Tara, Shepherd's behaviour wasn't your fault. I'm sure if you knew that things would play out that way, you wouldn't have left the way you did."

"But I did leave the way I did."

"He doesn't blame you, Tara. No one blames you."

I got up and walked to the window, pressing my hands to the glass. I hoped it would settle me, calm the blood rushing through my body.

"We waited a long time for him to come to his senses, to stop drinking. In the end, we ambushed him one morning at breakfast. We convinced him he needed to change. And he did. To everyone else, it looked like he had finally gotten over you and moved on. But I knew better. I saw the sadness in him, the loneliness, the loss."

The silence stretched. I finally realised that Sammy was waiting for me. To do something? To say something? I didn't know. I lifted my head.

"I don't know how long he'd been concocting this idea to win you back with a scavenger hunt. Three months ago, he shared it with me. There was nothing I could do to stop him. His mind was set."

"So, you helped him."

"I helped him. One way or another, he would finally have an answer. Either you wanted him or you didn't. Either answer would be a life saver."

I leaned against the glass hoping the coolness would steady my beating heart. "If he did all this to win me back, why did he leave?"

"He told me that it was a mistake, that you didn't love

him. That the prize and your foundation was at the top of your agenda."

Stupid. I should have tried harder to make him listen. "I thought I had time to convince him."

"As soon as I raised the three million dollars for your part of the prize, that was his cue."

"What are you talking about? What three million?"

"When he realised what the prize money meant to you, he thought the only way you could ever forgive him was if he raised the money for your foundation."

"Three million? He raised *three million*?" The glass at my back had no effect on me. I pressed myself harder against it. What I really needed was something to squeeze, to release my anger into.

"Yes. Even at the end when he thought all hope was lost, he made sure that money came to you. It was the last thing he could do for you. He was so scared to tell you, Tara. It was ridiculous."

The last thing he could do for me? The last bloody thing he could have done for me was listen to what I had to say. "Didn't you think this whole thing could have played out badly?"

"Obviously. Look at where we are now."

I glared at Sammy. He shifted in his seat.

"Sammy, he lied to me for days. His rule about staying together at all times—"

"I know. I'm sorry."

"I wondered how the hell I was paired with him out of all of the contestants. I had checked the set-up of the game thoroughly—it all checked out. So, I thought it was just a coincidence." I stood behind the lounge, grasping the top. Squeezing it for dear life. "But it was all *lies*."

"Not all of it. Not the way he feels about you."

That was the truth at least. Because the way I felt about him wasn't a lie.

"How did you ever think this was OK?"

"I didn't. But I didn't know what else to do. I hoped you'd both see reason in the end."

Words would not come.

"We may not understand completely the reasons he did this but it came from a genuine place. I'm telling you, when this started, he didn't for one moment think it was the wrong thing to do. Although, sometimes I wondered if he was thinking at all."

He was right, Shepherd was one of the most genuine people I knew. Even as my anger abated, I held onto the last slivers, hoping it would help drive me forward.

"Didn't you think my treasures were creative?" he asked.

"What?" His disarming tactic worked.

"The coin with your initials showing you were two sides of the same coin."

I shook my head at Sammy. "I'm furious with both of you."

"Come on, think about the treasures."

I sighed. What was the point? I couldn't be angry with Sammy. He was just looking out for his friend. In one of the stupidest ways possible, but still... "The ceramic ball. Our initials were on the inside..."

"Yeah, like when you two went zorbing."

"In the gardens and we ended up in the lake. That's why the ball was in the water."

"Exactly." Sammy grinned. He was proud of himself. I

shook my head, trying not to smile. "Now what about the locks?"

I paced the room. The locks. What about the locks?

"I don't know. The only thing I can think of is the Love Lock Bridge in Paris."

"The locks symbolised how you could unlock each other's hearts."

Well, that was achieved. "You put a lot of thought into this."

"The puppy certificate was in memory of Benny and how you told us you wanted a dog again one day."

Benny. Zac. The bundle of fur shoved in my face. I smiled. Oh, how much I would love another dog....one day.

I grabbed the coaster off the table and turned it over to the motto on the back: *Aletheuontes de en Agape.* "What does this mean?"

"Speaking the truth in love."

TWO WEEKS AFTER

Shepherd

DAD GAVE my shoulder a squeeze at the table before he joined me for breakfast. He rubbed the back of his neck and looked at me with concern in his eyes. His brown hair, the same shade as mine, was greying at his temples.

"It's OK, Dad. I'm not going to go off the deep end again."

"I'm sorry it didn't work out for you, Shep."

"Thanks, Dad. At least I know now."

"Son, I know you're hurting. It's written all over your face. I know there's nothing I can say to make you feel better."

Maria set our breakfast down in front of us. She patted my cheek before moving away.

"I need to keep busy at work. It will be better if I don't have a lot of time to think."

He nodded.

"I'd like to extend my clinics. I want to help people full time. Can we afford that?"

"We certainly can. Your great grandfather invested well. And what better way to use that money than to help people?"

I smiled at him.

"I'm proud of you, Shep. You're a compassionate man. You're strong in ways you don't even realise. You never complained about growing up without a mom."

"I had you and Maria. I didn't miss out on anything."

"But it's not only that. You've worked hard to be the best person you can be. And even though you knew the risk when you decided to win Tara back, you did it anyway. That's one of the bravest things someone could do, to put their heart out there like that."

Yet, I wasn't brave enough to tell her the truth about the game.

I loved my dad. He was always there for me. Even when he didn't know how to help me, he did. I wouldn't let him see me waste away. My heart might be broken but I wouldn't let it take me down with it. For the people I loved, I would make the best life I could without Tara.

He patted my shoulder before taking his plate to the sink. "I'll see you at work."

I SAT down at my desk. The pile of paperwork before me seemed to grow everyday, like a weed after some sun and rain. I looked through the file of my first client of the day. Mrs. Johnson. The County was trying to take her home away. They claimed it was old and dilapidated and had it condemned. What made it suspicious was that most of the houses around her had been sold to a developer. She resisted. Now, all of a sudden, her house was considered unsafe? Last week I'd sent an independent contractor to investigate the condition of her home. It was his report I was reading, complete with photos.

The house was in sound condition. There were two walls with rot, but they weren't load bearing walls. The rot would be easy to fix and posed no threat. In the initial County report, it dismissed the owner as a hoarder and stated it was infested with vermin. The photos confirmed that there were a lot of items in the small space but the report said there was no evidence of rodents.

This was a horrible display of bullying and intimidation.

A knock sounded at my door and Tiffany, my secretary, poked her head in. "Mrs Johnson is here. Shall I send her in?"

"Yes please."

I stood as Mrs Johnson walked in. She leant heavily on her walking stick. I walked around to the front of my desk and moved the visitor's chair backwards so she would be able to sit in it easier.

"Thank you, Mr Bell."

Normally I would get straight down to business but I felt Mrs Johnson should be able to tell her story. After all, everyone had a story to tell. And there should be someone willing to listen to it.

"Mrs Johnson, tell me about your home."

"Those men want to take it away from me. The County says it's unsafe."

"How long have you lived there?"

"Since the day I was born," she said, raising her chin with pride. "My Daddy was the first African American man in our neighbourhood to own a house. When he died, it was passed down to me and my husband. We weren't blessed with children, so when my husband passed it became mine alone. I find it hard sometimes to keep up with the maintenance."

"The County has condemned your home declaring the state of it has caused a vermin infestation and it's unsafe."

"That isn't true."

"I agree. The report from my investigator confirms that."

"What can I do? I have no money to fight the County."

"Don't worry about money. The service I provide is free."

Her toothy smile lit up her face. Her whole body seemed to lift. The change in her body language lifted my spirits.

"The first thing I'm going to do is request a stay. This will give us time to fix things."

"How much will that cost?"

"The two walls will cost $2,000 to repair."

She nodded. "I can afford that. But what about the hoarding?"

"That will be more difficult I think, due to your physical condition."

She nodded again. This would be something personal to her. She would want to take time which could hinder the process. It may have taken years to gather all of those belongings but she would most likely have two weeks to cull it down.

"I can help you. I can come after work and help you."

I sounded quite convincing, even to myself. I was convinced about one thing at least: it would keep my mind off Tara. The intense memories had yet to fade. Those many fateful words would enter my mind, usually when it was resting, or had a chance at quietness or emptiness. The best solution was to keep busy.

"Is this part of your service?"

"Not usually, but it will be a win-win. I can help you and the extra work will help me."

She studied me closely. Her eyes searched mine, roamed my face, and settled on my hands.

"OK."

THREE WEEKS AFTER

Tara

I KNEW I had to face the music. I had put off visiting Nan and Pop since the scavenger hunt ended.

Of course, we'd spoken, but I had always veered the conversation away from Shepherd. As I stood outside their small house in the retirement village, I steeled myself for what was to come. I could face down crime lords in Africa but facing two of the people I loved most in the world, knowing they would be disappointed, was something else. I knocked.

As the footsteps approached, my heart quickened. The door opened. Pop's eyes widened as he saw it was me, followed by a smile.

"Tara, love. We've missed you."

He pulled me into a firm hug before closing the door and ushering me to the lounge room. Nan looked up from the couch and almost leapt to her feet.

"Tara."

She came to me and embraced me. It was an embrace full

of love and understanding. When we let each other go, the hands that had healed me over the years rubbed my shoulders.

"Tell us what happened."

Pop made us all some hot chocolate. I sat at the table cradling the mug in my hands while I told them everything. The strength of what I felt for Shepherd, how life felt empty all over again.

I was angry when Sammy first told me about the fake hunt. But I couldn't stay angry for long. How could I? Not when Shepherd had put such thought into it. Not only to see me again but to raise the three million dollars.

"I can't believe he went to all of that effort. Why didn't he just call?" Nan said.

"I think only Shepherd can tell you that. He thought there was no other way."

"Well, you did leave in a big hurry. And you totally ignored any attempt he made to contact you."

"But you know why I left. I couldn't deal with losing him to drugs."

This was it. That was the gate opened for me to tell them. I tried to pull the strength I felt while with Shepherd to prepare myself. How do you start a conversation that you should have had six years ago? Start it with the name of the person you love, I guess. I was shaking.

"Shepherd said I should speak to you about Zac. About how I failed."

"Shepherd used those words, did he?" Pop's voice was hard.

"No, they are my choice of words. Shepherd said I did everything I could. And that you would forgive me, even though there was nothing to forgive."

"Tara, dear, what is there to forgive? There's no blame to lay here, but if there were, we are both as responsible as you."

I looked between them. How could they know what I was talking about and not blame me?

"But you don't understand. I should have called you and asked you for help. If I did Zac may not have died."

Pop took my hand. "And we should have come straight down when we knew something was not right."

"Tara, we knew something was going on. When he stopped joining you on the phone calls, we should have asked. We shouldn't have let you carry that burden on your own."

Oh God, all this time they felt the same way I did? I needed to stop hiding from having these hard conversations. Tears rolled silently down my cheeks. Nan took hold of my hand and rubbed it.

"We need to talk about Shepherd," she said. "There has been too much kept out of the open."

"What are you going to do?" Pop asked, always straight to the point.

"I'm going to give the money back."

"I'm not talking about the money, Tara."

"Tara, love, what are you going to do about Shepherd?" Nan asked.

"I'm going to give him the money back, in person."

"And then what?"

FIVE WEEKS AFTER

Shepherd

MRS. JOHNSON WAS A REAL TROOPER. Knowing that her home was on the line, she helped me late into every evening.

By the tenth day, we were nearly finished.

"Shepherd, will you tell me what you're hiding from?"

The question took me by surprise. We'd spoken a lot over the past ten days about her and Edgar and their life together. I spoke a bit about work, but that was about all.

"I'm not hiding from anything."

Mrs. Johnson glanced at me.

"Shepherd, I may be old, and my body may be faltering, but there is nothing wrong with my mind."

I placed a box of newspapers on the table for her to examine. "What would you like done with these?"

"Shepherd, you work seven days a week, from dawn until well after dark. Your mind isn't always here with me—"

"Mrs. Johnson—"

"Your eyes show a man consumed by sadness. Your face shows the tiredness of a man haunted—"

"Mrs. Johnson—"

"Shepherd, let me help you."

"Mrs. Johnson, what would you like done with these newspapers?"

"They belonged to Edgar. He kept them because he liked to look back to see how things have changed in the world. I don't need them."

I agreed. Looking back was not always healthy.

I picked up the box and took it to the recycling pile. I picked up another box and placed it on the table.

"Do you think all of this will make a difference? I'm one elderly woman trying to fight not only the County, but a giant corporation."

"I believe good will win over evil."

"Have you always had this blind faith?"

"It's better to have faith than to believe there's no hope."

"But for you, there's no hope in love."

No, there was no hope in love. Not without Tara. I took a deep breath. Talking about it brought the pain right to the surface.

"Not today."

"Tomorrow?"

"Unlikely."

"Ever?"

"I doubt it."

Sighing, I sat in the seat opposite her and told her everything. I even told her I knew Sammy had followed me to Sydney but he never uttered a word about it. If the trip had gone well, he wouldn't have held back.

"Shepherd, why didn't you let her explain?"

"What was there to explain?"

"You're willing to believe there is good in a world that's so cruel, and sure to destroy the weak, but you're not willing to believe in love?"

She looked at me while I stared back, not saying a word.

"So, you decided the best thing to do was leave without saying a word? You did to her exactly what she did to you five years ago."

The gentleness in her voice did not hide the bluntness of her words. It was like an MMA fighter had kicked me in the chest. That's exactly what I had done. How could I have done that to the person I loved most in the world?

"Let's finish off here," I said, standing and opening the box between us.

SIX WEEKS AFTER

Shepherd

I FINISHED my notes on Mrs. Johnson's file. It was a good day. Her house had been reinspected and was cleared. We'd been to court and the order was withdrawn. Mrs. Johnson could spend the rest of her years in her one and only home. Good won out again.

Tiffany, my assistant, opened the door and stepped in. As I looked up at her, she closed the door behind her, standing against it, her hands pressed to the wood behind her. Strange. It was time for her to leave for the day. Usually she'd just poke her head around the door to check if I needed anything before she left.

"Your last appointment is here."

"I don't have any more appointments today."

I looked at the calendar on my screen to double check.

When I looked back at Tiffany, she was still standing against the door, gazing down at the ground. Slowly, she raised her eyes to mine.

"Your dad asked me to squeeze her in. She needs help with a visa."

"OK, send her in."

I watched Tiffany as she left. When she passed the person walking in, she reached out her hand to give the other person's a squeeze. My eyes rose from their hands to the face of Tara.

My heart banged in my rib cage. I stood up.

"Tara."

"Hello, Shepherd."

My first instinct was to round the table, to take her in my arms, to kiss her. I defied that instinct. My feet stayed firm. "What are you doing here?"

"I came to return this."

She walked to the desk and placed something before me. It was a cheque for three million dollars.

"That's your money. For your foundation."

"I'd rather not start a future where I was indebted to someone."

"To me." I sank down in my chair. She was saying something but I wasn't paying any notice. "Two hundred thousand of that is yours."

"Shepherd." The crispness in her voice caught my attention.

I looked up from the cheque to her face. Her beautiful face.

"Are you listening to me?"

"No."

Sighing, she sat down in one of the chairs in front of the desk. When I made eye contact with her, she continued. "I don't want to start a future with you, knowing we owe so much money."

A future...with me? "What?"

"We should not start a life together so much in debt."

"Together?"

I must sound like an idiot.

"Yes, Shepherd, together."

"But I thought..."

"I know what you thought, but I couldn't speak to you. You had shut down. I thought we had more time together. I thought once you'd calmed down, I would be able to tell you that I was sorry and I never wanted to leave you, ever again."

I tried to absorb what she was saying. I heard all of the words. I repeated them to myself. She didn't want to leave?

"But you told your grandparents it didn't seem right and you couldn't because it was too hard. That you were only there for the three million. I heard you."

"You only heard part of the conversation. I was scared that you would never forgive me, that it would be too hard for you to trust me again. I'm still scared."

<hr>

Tara

I COULDN'T READ the emotion on Shepherd's face. Was his heart open enough to hear what I was saying? My hands were shoved between my legs to stop them from shaking. What was he thinking?

He stood up and made his way around the desk. When he was standing in front of me, he said, "I'm sorry, Tara."

A cold sweat broke out across my body. I prepared myself to stand up, like standing would help me fight for him, give me more power somehow. What was he saying sorry for? Had he had enough? I needed him to believe me. I didn't want to spend another day without him. I loved him with all of my being. I'd always loved him.

Shepherd turned the chair next to me so that it was facing mine and sat down. My heart beat fast. He moved closer so that his knees were on either side of mine. I waited for his words, cold dread in my stomach.

He passed a hand over his face.

"I was so scared that you were going to leave again. I ran."

I reached my sweaty hand out to his. My heart was in my throat as I waited for him to take my hand. My fear was tangible. Still, I waited. Vulnerable. Alone.

He took hold of my hand.

"I'm sorry, Shepherd. I'm sorry for everything. I understand if you can't trust me."

I searched his face. His fingers slipped out of mine before rubbing the back of his neck, messing up his hair. He leant back in his chair. My heart dropped. Pulling my hand back, I stared down at it.

"I want to trust you. But the thought of you leaving and me hitting rock bottom, I don't think I can do that again."

"I'm sorry, Shepherd. Sammy told me everything, all the pain I'd caused, how much torment you went through. I'll keep saying sorry every day for the rest of my life, until you believe me."

"This wasn't your fault, Tara. There were a thousand different ways I could have dealt with you leaving. I didn't need to choose the path I did."

Reaching my hand out, I rested it against his cheek. What had I done? My selfishness, my warped need to protect myself, broke this amazing man. And for five years he'd held onto my memory, always holding a sliver of hope for us. I hated myself for my actions.

Slowly his eyes made their way to mine.

"I love you, Tara. I wanted you. No, I needed you. Sometimes I thought maybe when we reunited, I might figure out that the perfect memory I had of you was a fallacy. It wasn't. You were even more perfect. I fell for you, all over again."

"I never stopped loving you, Shepherd. I just couldn't bear to lose you, to watch you die. I thought staying away would be easier. In one way it was, but part of my heart was always missing. I was incomplete."

"What about your foundation?"

"You are more important than my foundation."

Movement sounded outside the door. Shepherd looked at it, his eyes narrowing.

"It's probably Sammy or your dad."

"What are they doing here?"

"Why don't you go ask them?"

Shepherd stood and strode to the door. His shoulders rose and fell as he took a deep breath. Opening the door, he ushered them in. They stood inside the office looking between us. Tiffany stood on the threshold.

"Have you two sorted your shit out?" Sammy asked.

I couldn't help smiling.

"Not yet."

"Do you need some help?" Shepherd's dad asked.

"We could help you talk through things," Tiffany offered.

"We're doing OK," I said. And I honestly thought we were. It was good that we were talking; finally, being open.

"Are you actually talking things through?" Sammy asked, staring us both down. "That's been your problem all along."

"Yes, we're talking," Shepherd said, shaking his head, bemused at his best friend. "You can go. We don't need a babysitter."

"Have you told him yet how *stupid* his scavenger hunt idea was?"

"We hadn't got to that part."

Shepherd turned to me. "Stupid?"

"Well, you have to admit, going to such lengths to win a girl back is over the top. A phone call would have been a good start."

"I'm devo," he said, holding his hand over his heart.

Sammy laughed without reservation.

Shepherd's dad moved towards Sammy, getting ready to leave with him. Sammy made no attempt to move. He looked between us. "If I find out you two haven't worked things out, I'll lock you in a room together with me as mediator."

"Oooh, we're scared," Shepherd said.

I bit my lip to keep my laughter in. Tiffany didn't hold back; she openly laughed.

"Don't test me, Shepherd," Sammy said as he walked out of the office.

***

Shepherd

I TURNED BACK TO TARA. Her smile melted the tenseness in my muscles away.

"You know he's serious, right?"

She nodded.

"It was really hard for Sammy and my dad."

She reached for my hand as I sat next to her. Just her touch calmed my nerves. I wanted to lean over and kiss her, to feel her soft lips, to taste her. I held back. We had a lot to talk about, and kissing her would put a stop to any talking because once I started, I wouldn't be able to stop.

"It was bad, Tara. I was lost for a long time."

Her hand stroked mine, willing me to talk.

"They talked me straight. I knew I needed to clean up, to make you proud, them, me."

"I am proud, Shepherd. You are an amazing, selfless person."

She leant forward and kissed my lips tenderly, resting her forehead against mine as her lips drew away.

"I'm never going back there. Even if you said to me today that you couldn't do this, I wouldn't go back to the person I became."

She kissed me again, gently, quickly, before sitting up.

"I'm not going anywhere. You're everything to me."

That night of our last hunt dragged itself into my mind. Not really dragged, it's not like I'd forgotten about it. It was always at the forefront of my mind. Reminding me. Taunting me.

"That night, on our last hunt, you told one of the ladies that I wasn't your boyfriend."

"You obviously missed the part where I said you were the love of my life." Her answer was instant, like she had been thinking of that night, too.

There it goes again. Another punch to the chest. Fuck.

All of this because I was too scared to even talk.

"Yes, I did miss that."

"We can't keep doing this. We need to talk when we're scared."

"I know. I fucked this up."

"We both did. I should have made you listen. I shouldn't have waited."

I held her hand tighter, never wanting to let her go again. As if she read my mind, she said, "I don't ever want to leave you again. Everything I do from this day, I want to do with you."

I smiled. That's what I wanted, too. She hopped onto my lap and took my face between her hands, kissing me, whispering words of love between kisses. I was instantly hard. As my dick strained towards her, a smile appeared, even as her soft lips caressed mine.

Pulling away, she said, "Let's go home."

"Home?"

"Yeah, you know, where you live."

"Smart arse." I gave her butt a slap as she stood up.

"Maria has dinner cooking for us."

When I looked at her blankly, she said, "Do you think I did all this by myself? My things were sent over weeks ago. Your dad has set up the guest house for us."

"Weeks ago?"

"Took a while to get my temporary visa sorted."

"Ah, so the visa story Tiffany gave me wasn't a lie."

"No. If you want me to stay, you're going to have to help me get a permanent one."

"You seem pretty confident that I would, seeing as you sent your things over," I teased.

"Let's just say that your dad and Sammy were confident." She gave me a crooked smile.

"I'll work on it first thing tomorrow."

Her smile lit up the room and my heart. There was no way I could go home and sit through a family meal before ravishing her body. I walked past her and locked the door. Her wide eyes swung to mine. I pulled her into my arms.

Without hesitation, she pressed herself into me. I went even harder. My mouth claimed hers. Her hands fumbled as she unbuttoned my jeans. Her hand found my dick. I moaned into her mouth as she slid her hand down my shaft and rubbed my balls. If I didn't move fast, it would be over before I even began.

I pulled her shorts down and my hand reached between her legs. She was wet already. Everything about her drove me insane, but that wetness, knowing it was for me, made me want her more. I pushed her towards my desk, stepping out of my jeans on the way. Pushing Tara down, I slipped into her in one fluid movement. It felt so good as she claimed me. Part of my mind said to go slow. My resolve wasn't that strong. I bent to meet her mouth as she wrapped her legs around me. Each gasp and moan from her lips drove me harder. Tara moaned my name as she clenched around me, sending me over the edge.

As I stood up, she grinned up at me. I took all of her in as she lay before me.

"At least we'll be able to enjoy dinner now."

I laughed as I pulled her up and gave her another kiss.

SIX MONTHS AFTER

Tara

I PROPPED myself onto my elbows and looked at Shepherd. Waking up beside him every day made me smile. Going to sleep beside him made me smile. Everything about him made me smile.

"Shepherd, we need to get up. We have somewhere to go."

He raised his eyebrows. "Where do we have to go?"

"I'm not telling you. It's a celebratory gift for us, for my dual citizenship being approved."

"And we have to go *now*? I don't even have time to ravish your body?"

Just the thought of having sex with him made my nipples hard. He took my pause as an invitation, swiftly rolling me onto my back, hooking his fingers into my underwear, and then pulling them down within a millisecond.

"Well I guess I can't deny you now."

His mouth crushed mine into silence. Would I ever get enough of him? As he pushed himself into me, I gasped. His mouth slid down my neck, kissing and nipping along the way before settling in the spot between my neck and shoulder. He rocked between my legs, long strokes, taking his time, enjoying every moment. Shepherd kissed me long and slow and as his movements changed to thrusts, I moaned his name into his mouth. He released my lips. His quickening breath against my neck had the same effect it always did. I drove my hips to meet his, clutching his back. I wanted to hold the orgasm back, to ride it out, but there was no stopping it. I clenched around him, a cry escaping my mouth as my back arched. He came in almost the same instant, filling me, groaning and stiffening until he was completely spent.

"Worth three million dollars?" I asked.

"Every last cent."

He kissed me firmly before swinging his legs out of bed. I followed him to the shower.

"COME ON, we're going to be late," I said, pulling Shepherd along.

"It's not my fault you're so horny."

"Like you can talk."

Shepherd grinned as he saw the sign for the local dog rescue. I kissed him quickly at the door before pulling him inside. He raised his eyebrows at me when we reached the counter.

"Surprise," I said.

He just smiled at me ruefully as a lady approached us. Her badge indicated she was the manager, and she gave him a broad smile and shook his hand.

"Shepherd, so nice to see you again."

I'm sure my eyes opened so wide my brows almost met my hairline.

"Surprise," he said. "We're getting a dog."

I was speechless as I looked between him and the manager. He gave me a quick kiss.

"Your wife is as beautiful as you said," the manager chimed in, taking my arm as my faced reddened. "Shepherd said you would likely want an older dog."

I nodded, still not able to formulate words. We stopped at every cage, peering at the beautiful faces looking back. Some were so excited they bound to the door, their tails and bodies wagging. Others lay on their beds, lifting their heads, studying us. One sat about a metre from the gate, not moving as we approached. I read the name on the door, George.

"This is George. He is our long-term resident."

I crouched down at the gate, so I was on the same level as George.

"How long has he been here?" Shepherd asked, as he lowered himself beside me.

"Two hundred and eighty-two days."

George looked between us, his eyes a mixture of brown and amber.

"Why so long?"

"He's quite reserved. And big."

I stood up, not taking my eyes off George. "Can we go in to meet him?"

"Sure." The manager opened the gate for us.

Shepherd was right beside me as I crouched down again. George's eyes never left us, his mouth widening into a smile. Still, he sat.

"Hi, George," Shepherd and I said in unison.

That was it. The spell was broken. George stood and in one bound he was before us, his tail wagging. I didn't even get a chance to introduce myself before his face was in mine, his wet nose against my cheek. He shared that nose between Shepherd and I. Turning 360 degrees he stamped his feet, his whole body dancing with excitement.

"Well, I'll be," the manager said behind us.

I stood beside Shepherd, leaning into him and giving him a quick kiss. George sat at our feet, his big brown eyes staring up at us. Shepherd turned to the manager and said, "We'll take him."

***

Shepherd

GEORGE SAT IN THE BACK, his head between ours in the front seat, as we sat in the carpark.

"I have another surprise for you. Close your eyes," I said.

Tara looked at me, her mouth tilted up on one side.

"Close your eyes," I repeated. She complied, a nervous grin on her face. I dropped a set of keys into her hand.

Tara opened her eyes and examined the keys. Then read the tag. "Zachariah Hill Foundation."

Her eyes glistened as they looked up at mine.

"Your first outreach van. The people who donated initially stand by their donation. You will have money to run it."

She looked back down at the keys before returning her eyes to mine.

"You didn't fail Zac, Tara. You were there with him until the last minute when many others would have given up."

"Oh, Shepherd." She practically launched herself across the car and embraced my lips with hers.

"You made all of my dreams come true. The least I could do is help with yours."

THANK YOU for reading my novel.

BOOK REVIEWS from awesome readers like you are the lifeblood of authors, especially new authors. Reviews help readers find new books and authors find new readers. They don't need to be long or detailed, even two sentence reviews add value.

It would be appreciated if you could leave a review here:

Amazon

Goodreads

BookBub

OTHER books available in the Love Down Under Series are:

<u>The Cat's Out of the Bag</u>

One van. Two hearts. Thousands of kilometres.

Jesse's a self-made billionaire who yearns to get away from his empty life and the money-hungry parasites who inhabit it. The plan? Go to Australia, tell no one about his money and find himself. Instead of finding just himself, he finds Evie, who is everything anyone should aspire to be. Now, what he aspires to be, is hers. But to be hers, he needs to tell her everything.

Evie has left her past behind. She has rebuilt herself, and her life, into one of happiness. After she meets Jesse, while volunteering at a cat shelter, memories of her past filter back in. She is stronger now and wants to trust him. But after all she has been through, is trust even possible?

The quest to find a cat a forever home leads them to travel across the country together. Can the close quarters drive them to open up to each other? Or will it drive them apart?

When two opposites collide, will their differences ignite a spark or send them into turmoil?

Frankie and Sebastian live totally different lives. Lives that are entwined through polo, the sport of kings.

Frankie's a country girl, working hard toward her dream of turning the family farm around. She needs to endure one more polo season to make that happen. She has no interest in high society or the rich, arrogant riders she has to deal with, especially Sebastian. Her heart may be softening to his charm, openness and love of working with horses, but her brain won't be convinced. She looks forward to her summer break on the farm, away from him, until her parents decide to invite Sebastian to stay.

Sebastian descends from royalty. Rich and arrogant come with his family title. But that status is something he'd rather avoid, just like he avoids returning home to a life he doesn't want. Sebastian sees a freedom in Frankie he wishes he had. Her life is full of love, family and horses; something he can only dream of. And her, he can dream of her. But a dream is all it will be, seeing as Frankie does her best to avoid him.

If only he can convince her to look past his title, and see that his hopes and dreams aren't so different from hers.

KEEP IN TOUCH

To be notified of future releases, and to keep up to date with other news, please join my newsletter.

https://www.subscribepage.com/p9p9yo

ACKNOWLEDGMENTS

Cover by Charmaine Ross Cover Designs
Edited by Salt & Sage Books
Proofread by Claerie Kavanagh
And thanks to my amazing beta readers

ABOUT THE AUTHOR

Cynthia is a project officer by day and a writer by night. She enjoys writing about places she visited with her daughter while they travelled around Australia. She says that travel and reading are the best educators. Still, to this day, they both enjoy travelling and reading. A love of animals sees them feature in her books, some have small parts, others larger.

Find her online: http://cynthiaterelst.com/

All of her social links can be found here, Linktree: https://linktr.ee/cynthiaterelst